Mrs. Raffl

Being the Adventures of an Ama

John Kendrick Bangs

Alpha Editions

This edition published in 2023

ISBN : 9789357955843

Design and Setting By
Alpha Editions
www.alphaedis.com
Email - info@alphaedis.com

Contents

Contents

I
THE ADVENTURE OF THE *HERALD* PERSONAL

That I was in a hard case is best attested by the fact that when I had paid for my Sunday *Herald* there was left in my purse just one tuppence-ha'penny stamp and two copper cents, one dated 1873, the other 1894. The mere incident that at this hour eighteen months later I can recall the dates of these coins should be proof, if any were needed, of the importance of the coppers in my eyes, and therefore of the relative scarcity of funds in my possession. Raffles was dead—killed as you may remember at the battle of Spion Kop— and I, his companion, who had never known want while his deft fingers were able to carry out the plans of that insinuating and marvellous mind of his, was now, in the vernacular of the American, up against it. I had come to the United States, not because I had any liking for that country or its people, who, to tell the truth, are too sharp for an ordinary burglar like myself, but because with the war at an end I had to go somewhere, and English soil was not safely to be trod by one who was required for professional reasons to evade the eagle eye of Scotland Yard until the Statute of Limitations began to have some bearing upon his case. That last affair of Raffles and mine, wherein we had successfully got away with the diamond stomacher of the duchess of Herringdale, was still a live matter in British detective circles, and the very audacity of the crime had definitely fastened the responsibility for it upon our shoulders. Hence it was America for me, where one could be as English as one pleased without being subject to the laws of his Majesty, King Edward VII., of Great Britain and Ireland and sundry other possessions upon which the sun rarely if ever sets. For two years I had led a precarious existence, not finding in the land of silk and money quite as many of those opportunities to add to the sum of my prosperity as the American War Correspondent I had met in the Transvaal led me to expect. Indeed, after six months of successful lecturing on the subject of the Boers before various lyceums in the country, I was reduced to a state of penury which actually drove me to thievery of the pettiest and most vulgar sort. There was little in the way of mean theft that I did not commit. During the coal famine, for instance, every day passing the coal-yards to and fro, I would appropriate a single piece of the precious anthracite until I had come into possession of a scuttleful, and this I would sell to the suffering poor at prices varying from three shillings to two dollars and a half—a precarious living indeed. The only respite I received for six months was in the rape of the hansom-cab, which I successfully carried through one bitter cold night in January. I hired the vehicle at Madison Square and drove to a small tavern on the Boston Post

Road, where the icy cold of the day gave me an excuse for getting my cabby drunk in the guise of kindness. Him safely disposed of in a drunken stupor, I drove his jaded steed back to town, earned fifteen dollars with him before daybreak, and then, leaving the cab in the Central Park, sold the horse for eighteen dollars to a snow-removal contractor over on the East Side. It was humiliating to me, a gentleman born, and a partner of so illustrious a person as the late A. J. Raffles, to have to stoop to such miserable doings to keep body and soul together, but I was forced to confess that, whatever Raffles had left to me in the way of example, I was not his equal either in the conception of crime or in the nerve to carry a great enterprise through. My biggest coups had a way of failing at their very beginning—which was about the only blessing I enjoyed, since none of them progressed far enough to imperil my freedom, and, lacking confederates, I was of course unable to carry through the profitable series of abductions in the world of High Finance that I had contemplated. Hence my misfortunes, and now on this beautiful Sunday morning, penniless but for the coppers and the postage-stamp, with no breakfast in sight, and, fortunately enough, not even an appetite, I turned to my morning paper for my solace.

"THIS I WOULD SELL TO THE SUFFERING POOR"

Running my eye up and down the personal column, which has for years been my favorite reading of Sunday mornings, I found the usual assortment of matrimonial enterprises recorded: pathetic appeals from P. D. to meet Q. on the corner of Twenty-third Street at three; imploring requests from J. A. K. to return at once to "His Only Mother," who promises to ask no questions; and finally—could I believe my eyes now riveted upon the word?—my own sobriquet, printed as boldly and as plainly as though I were some patent cure for all known human ailments. It seemed incredible, but there it was beyond all peradventure:

"WANTED.—A Butler. BUNNY preferred. Apply to Mrs. A. J. Van Raffles, Bolivar Lodge, Newport, R.I."

To whom could that refer if not to myself, and what could it mean? Who was this Mrs. A. J. Van Raffles?—a name so like that of my dead friend that it seemed almost identical. My curiosity was roused to concert pitch. If this strange advertiser should be— But no, she would not send for me after that stormy interview in which she cast me over to take the hand of Raffles: the brilliant, fascinating Raffles, who would have won his Isabella from Ferdinand, Chloe from her Corydon, Pierrette from Pierrot—ay, even Heloise from Abelard. I never could find it in my heart to blame Henriette for losing her heart to him, even though she had already promised it to me, for I myself could not resist the fascination of the man at whose side I faithfully worked even after he had stolen from me this dearest treasure of my heart. And yet who else could it be if not the lovely Henriette? Surely the combination of Raffles, with or without the Van, and Bunny was not so usual as to permit of so remarkable a coincidence.

"I will go to Newport at once," I cried, rising and pacing the floor excitedly, for I had many times, in cursing my loneliness, dreamed of Henriette, and had oftener and oftener of late found myself wondering what had become of her, and then the helplessness of my position burst upon me with full force. How should I, the penniless wanderer in New York, get to Bolivar Lodge at Newport? It takes money in this sordid country to get about, even as it does in Britain—in sorry truth, things in detail differ little whether one lives under a king or a president; poverty is quite as hard to bear, and free passes on the railroad are just as scarce.

"Curses on these plutocrats!" I muttered, as I thought of the railway directors rolling in wealth, running trains filled with empty seats to and from the spot that might contain my fortune, and I unable to avail myself of them for the lack of a paltry dollar or two. But suddenly the thought flashed over me— telegraph collect. If it is she, she will respond at once.

And so it was that an hour later the following message was ticked over the wires:

"Personal to-day's *Herald* received. Telegraph railway fare and I will go to you instantly.

(Signed),
BUNNY."

For three mortal hours I paced the streets feverishly awaiting the reply, and at two-thirty it came, disconcerting enough in all conscience:

"If you are not a bogus Bunny you will know how to raise the cash. If you are a bogus Bunny I don't want you."

It was simple, direct, and convincing, and my heart fluttered like the drum-beat's morning call to action the moment I read it.

"THE WHOLE CONTENTS AND THE PLATTER AS WELL FELL AT MY FEET"

"By Jove!" I cried. "The woman is right, of course. It must be Henriette, and I'll go to her if I have to rob a nickel-in-the-slot machine."

It was as of old. Faint-hearted I always was until some one gave me a bit of encouragement. A word of praise or cheer from Raffles in the old days and

I was ready to batter down Gibraltar, a bit of discouragement and a rag was armor-plate beside me.

"'If you are not a bogus Bunny you will know,'" I read, spreading the message out before me. "That is to say, *she* believes that if I am really myself I can surmount the insurmountable. Gad! I'll do it." And I set off hot-foot up Fifth Avenue, hoping to discover, or by cogitation in the balmy air of the spring-time afternoon, to conceive of some plan to relieve my necessities. But, somehow or other, it wouldn't come. There were no pockets about to be picked in the ordinary way. I hadn't the fare for a ride on the surface or elevated cars, where I might have found an opportunity to relieve some traveller of his purse, and as for snatching such a thing from some shopper, it was Sunday and the women who would have been an easy prey on a bargain-day carried neither purse nor side-bag with them. I was in despair, and then the pealing bells of St. Jondy's, the spiritual home of the multi-millionaires of New York, rang out the call to afternoon service. It was like an invitation—the way was clear. My plan was laid in an instant, and it worked beyond my most hopeful anticipations. Entering the church, I was ushered to a pew about halfway up the centre aisle—despite my poverty, I had managed to keep myself always well-groomed, and no one would have guessed, to look at my faultless frock-coat and neatly creased trousers, at my finely gloved hand and polished top-hat, that my pockets held scarcely a brass farthing. The service proceeded. A good sermon on the Vanity of Riches found lodgment in my ears, and then the supreme moment came. The collection-plate was passed, and, gripping my two pennies in my hand, I made as if to place them in the salver, but with studied awkwardness I knocked the alms-platter from the hands of the gentleman who passed it. The whole contents and the platter as well fell at my feet, and from my lips in reverent whispers poured forth no end of most abject apologies. Of course I assisted in recovering the fallen bills and coins, and in less time than it takes to tell it the vestryman was proceeding on his way up the aisle, gathering in the contributions from other generously disposed persons as he went, as unconsciously as though the *contretemps* had never occurred, and happily unaware that out of the moneys cast to the floor by my awkward act two yellow-backed fifty-dollar bills, five half-dollars, and a dime remained behind under the hassock at my feet, whither I had managed to push them with my toe while offering my apologies.

An hour later, having dined heartily at Delsherrico's, I was comfortably napping in a Pullman car on my way to the Social Capital of the United States.

II
THE ADVENTURE OF THE NEWPORT VILLA

There is little need for me to describe in detail the story of my railway journey from New York to Newport. It was uneventful and unproductive save as to the latter end of it, when, on the arrival of the train at Wickford, observing that the prosperous-looking gentleman bound for Boston who occupied the seat next mine in the Pullman car was sleeping soundly, I exchanged my well-worn covert coat for his richly made, sable-lined surtout, and made off as well with his suit-case on the chance of its holding something that might later serve some one of my many purposes. I mention this in passing only because the suit-case, containing as it did all the essential features of a gentleman's evening attire, even to three superb pearl studs in the bosom of an immaculately white shirt, all of them, marvellously enough, as perfectly fitting as though they had been made for me, with a hundred unregistered first-mortgage bonds of the United States Steel Company—of which securities there will be more anon—enabled me later to appear before Mrs. Van Raffles in a guise so prosperous as to win an immediate renewal of her favor.

"We shall be almost as great a combination as the original Bunny," she cried, enthusiastically, when I told her of this coup. "With my brains and your blind luck nothing can stop us."

My own feelings as I drove up to Bolivar Lodge were mixed. I still loved Henriette madly, but the contrast between her present luxury and my recent misery grated harshly upon me. I could not rid myself of the notion that Raffles had told her of the secret hiding-place of the diamond stomacher of the duchess of Herringdale, and that she had appropriated to her own use all the proceeds of its sale, leaving me, who had risked my liberty to obtain it, without a penny's worth of dividend for my pains. It did not seem quite a level thing to do, and I must confess that I greeted the lady in a reproachful spirit. It was, indeed, she, and more radiantly beautiful than ever—a trifle thinner perhaps, and her eyes more coldly piercing than seductively winning as of yore, but still Henriette whom I had once so madly loved and who had jilted me for a better man.

"Dear old Bunny!" she murmured, holding out both hands in welcome. "Just to think that after all these years and in a strange land and under such circumstances we should meet again!"

"It is strange," said I, my eye roving about the drawing-room, which from the point of view of its appointments and decoration was about the richest thing I had ever seen either by light of day or in the mysterious glimpses one gets with a dark lantern of the houses of the moneyed classes. "It seems more than strange," I added, significantly, "to see you surrounded by such luxury.

A so-called lodge built of the finest grade of Italian marble; gardens fit for the palace of a king; a retinue of servants such as one scarcely finds on the ducal estates of the proudest families of England and a mansion that is furnished with treasures of art, any one of which is worth a queen's ransom."

"I do not wonder you are surprised," she replied, looking about the room with a smile of satisfaction that did little to soothe my growing wrath.

"It certainly leaves room for explanation," I retorted, coldly. "Of course, if Raffles told you where the Herringdale jewels were hid and you have disposed of them, some of all this could be accounted for; but what of me? Did it ever occur to you that I was entitled to some part of the swag?"

"Oh, you poor, suspicious old Bunny," she rippled. "Haven't I sent for you to give you some share of this—although truly you don't deserve it, for *this* is all mine. I haven't any more notion what became of the Herringdale jewels than the duchess of Herringdale herself."

"What?" I cried. "Then these surroundings—"

"Are self-furnishing," she said, with a merry little laugh, "and all through a plan of my own, Bunny. This house, as you may not be aware, is the late residence of Mr. and Mrs. Constant Scrappe—"

"Who are suing each other for divorce," I put in, for I knew of the Constant Scrappes in social life, as who did not, since a good third of the society items of the day concerned themselves with the matrimonial difficulties of this notable couple.

"Precisely," said Henriette. "Now Mrs. Scrappe is in South Dakota establishing a residence, and Colonel Scrappe is at Monte Carlo circulating his money with the aid of a wheel and a small ball. Bolivar Lodge, with its fine collection of old furniture, its splendid jades, its marvellous Oriental potteries, paintings, and innumerable small silver articles, is left here at Newport and for rent. What more natural, dear, than that I, needing a residence whose occupancy would in itself be an assurance of my social position, should snap it up with an eagerness which in this Newport atmosphere amounted nearly to a betrayal of plebeian origin?"

"But it must cost a fortune!" I cried, gazing about me at the splendors of the room, which even to a cursory inspection revealed themselves as of priceless value. "That cloisonné jar over by the fireplace is worth two hundred pounds alone."

"That is just the reason why I wanted this particular house, Bunny. It is also why I need your assistance in maintaining it," Mrs. Raffles returned.

"Woman is ever a mystery," I responded, with a harsh laugh. "Why in Heaven's name you think I can help you to pay your rent—"

"It is only twenty-five hundred dollars a month, Bunny," she said.

My answer was a roar of derisive laughter.

"Hear her!" I cried, addressing the empty air. "Only twenty-five hundred dollars a month! Why, my dear Henriette, if it were twenty-five hundred clam-shells a century I couldn't help you pay a day's rental, I am that strapped. Until this afternoon I hadn't seen thirty cents all at once for nigh on to six months. I have been so poor that I've had to take my morning coffee at midnight from the coffee-wagons of the New York, Boston, and Chicago sporting papers. In eight months I have not tasted a table-d'hôte dinner that an expert would value at fifteen cents net, and yet you ask me to help you pay twenty-five hundred dollars a month rent for a Newport palace! You must be mad."

"You are the same loquacious old Bunny that you used to be," said Mrs. Raffles, sharply, yet with a touch of affection in her voice. "You can't keep your trap shut for a second, can you? Do you know, Bunny, what dear old A. J. said to me just before he went to South Africa? It was that if you were as devoted to business as you were to words you'd be a wonder. His exact remark was that we would both have to look out for you for fear you would queer the whole business. Raffles estimated that your habit of writing-up full accounts of his various burglaries for the London magazines had made the risks one hundred per cent. bigger and the available swag a thousand per cent. harder to get hold of. 'Harry,' said he the night before he sailed, 'if I die over in the Transvaal and you decide to continue the business, get along as long as you can without a press-agent. If you go on the stage, surround yourself with 'em, but in the burglary trade they are a nuisance.'"

My answer was a sulky shrug of the shoulders.

"You haven't given me a chance to explain how you are to help me. I don't ask you for money, Bunny. Four dollars' worth of obedience is all I want," she continued. "The portable property in this mansion is worth about half a million dollars, my lad, and I want you to be—well, my official porter. I took immediate possession of this house, and my first month's rent was paid with the proceeds of a sale of three old bedsteads I found on the top floor, six pieces of Sèvres china from the southeast bedroom on the floor above this, and a Satsuma vase which I discovered in a hall-closet on the third floor."

A light began to dawn on me.

"Before coming here I eked out a miserable existence in New York as buyer for an antique dealer on Fourth Avenue," she explained. "He thinks I am still working for him, travelling about the country in search of bargains in high-boys, mahogany desks, antique tables, wardrobes, bedsteads—in short, valuable junk generally. Now do you see?"

"As Mrs. Raffles—or Van Raffles, as you have it now?" I demanded.

"Oh, Bunny, Bunny, Bunny! What a stupid you are! Never! As Miss Pratt-Robinson," she replied. "From this I earn fifteen dollars a week. The sources of the material I send him—well—do you see now, Bunny?"

"It is growing clearer," said I. "You contemplate paying the rent of this house with its contents, is that it?"

"What beautiful intelligence you have, Bunny!" she laughed, airily. "You know a hawk from a hand-saw. Nobody can pass a motor-car off on you for a horse, can they, Bunny dear? Not while you have that eagle eye of yours wide open. Yes, sir. That is the scheme. *I am going to pay the rental of this mansion with its contents.* Half a million dollars' worth of contents means how long at twenty-five hundred dollars a month? Eh?"

"Gad! Henriette," I cried. "You are worthy of Raffles, I swear it. You can be easy about your rent for sixteen years."

"That is about the size of it, as these Newport people have it," said Mrs. Raffles, beaming upon me.

"I'm still in the dark as to where I come in," said I.

"Promise to obey my directions implicitly," said Henriette "and you will receive your share of the booty."

"Henriette—" I cried, passionately, seizing her hand.

"No—Bunny—not now," she remonstrated, gently. "This is no time for sentiment. Just promise to obey, the love and honor business may come later."

"I will," said I.

"Well, then," she resumed, her color mounting high, and speaking rapidly, "you are to return at once to New York, taking with you three trunks which I have already packed, containing one of the most beautiful collections of jade ornaments that has ever been gathered together. You will rent a furnished apartment in some aristocratic quarter. Spread these articles throughout your rooms as though you were a connoisseur, and on Thursday next when Mr. Harold Van Gilt calls upon you to see your collection you will sell it to him for not less than eight thousand dollars."

"Aha!" said I. "I see the scheme."

"This you will immediately remit to me here," she continued, excitedly. "Mr. Van Gilt will pay cash."

I laughed. "Why eight thousand?" I demanded. "Are you living beyond your—ah—income?"

"No," she answered, "but next month's rent is due Tuesday, and I owe my servants and tradesmen twenty-five hundred dollars more."

"Even then there will be three thousand dollars over," I put in.

"True, Bunny, true. But I shall need it all, dear. I am invited to the P. J. D. Gasters on Sunday afternoon to play bridge," Henriette explained. "We must prepare for emergencies."

I returned to New York on the boat that night, and by Wednesday was safely ensconced in very beautifully furnished bachelor quarters near Gramercy Square, where on Thursday Mr. Harold Van Gilt called to see my collection of jades which I was selling because of a contemplated five-year journey into the East. On Friday Mr. Van Gilt took possession of the collection, and that night a check for eight thousand dollars went to Mrs. Van Raffles at Newport. Incidentally, I passed two thousand dollars to my own credit. As I figured it out, if Van Gilt was willing to pay ten thousand dollars for the stuff, and Henriette was willing to take eight thousand dollars for it, nobody was the loser by my pocketing two thousand dollars—unless, perhaps, it was Mr. and Mrs. Constant Scrappe who owned the goods. But that was none of my affair. I played straight with the others, and that was all there was to it as far as I was concerned.

III
THE ADVENTURE OF MRS. GASTER'S MAID

Two days after my bargain with Mr. Harold Van Gilt, in which he acquired possession of the Scrappe jades and Mrs. Van Raffles and I shared the proceeds of the ten thousand dollars check, I was installed at Bolivar Lodge as head-butler and steward, my salary to consist of what I could make out of it on the side, plus ten per cent. of the winnings of my mistress. It was not long before I discovered that the job was a lucrative one. From various tradesmen of the town I received presents of no little value in the form sometimes of diamond scarf-pins, gold link sleeve-buttons, cases of fine wines for my own use, and in one or two instances checks of substantial value. There was also what was called a steward's rebate on the monthly bills, which in circles where lavish entertainment is the order of the day amounted to a tidy little income in itself. My only embarrassment lay in the contact into which I was necessarily brought with other butlers, with whom I was perforce required to associate. This went very much against the grain at first, for, although I am scarcely more than a thief after all, I am an artistic one, and still retain the prejudice against inferior associations which an English gentleman whatever the vicissitudes of his career can never quite rid himself of. I had to join their club—an exclusive organization of butlers and "gentlemen's gentlemen"—otherwise valets—and in order to quiet all suspicion of my real status in the Van Raffles household I was compelled to act the part in a fashion which revolted me. Otherwise the position was pleasant, and, as I have intimated, more than lucrative.

It did not take me many days to discover that Henriette was a worthy successor to her late husband. Few opportunities for personal profit escaped her eye, and I was able to observe as time went on and I noted the accumulation of spoons, forks, nutcrackers, and gimcracks generally that she brought home with her after her calls upon or dinners with ladies of fashion that she had that quality of true genius which never overlooks the smallest details.

The first big coup after my arrival, as the result of her genius, was in the affair of Mrs. Gaster's maid. Henriette had been to a bridge afternoon at Mrs. Gaster's and upon her return manifested an extraordinary degree of excitement. Her color was high, and when she spoke her voice was tremulous. Her disturbed condition was so evident that my heart sank into my boots, for in our business nerve is a *sine qua non* of success, and it looked to me as if Henriette was losing hers. She has probably lost at cards to-day, I thought, and it has affected her usual calmness. I must do something to warn her against this momentary weakness. With this idea in mind, when the opportunity presented itself later I spoke.

"You lost at bridge to-day, Henriette," I said.

"Yes," she replied. "Twenty-five hundred dollars in two hours. How did you guess?"

"By your manner," said I. "You are as nervous as a young girl at a commencement celebration. This won't do, Henriette. Nerves will prove your ruin, and if you can't stand your losses at bridge, what will you do in the face of the greater crisis which in our profession is likely to confront us in the shape of an unexpected visit of police at any moment?"

Her answer was a ringing laugh.

"You absurd old rabbit," she murmured. "As if I cared about my losses at bridge! Why, my dear Bunny, I lost that money on purpose. You don't suppose that I am going to risk my popularity with these Newport ladies by winning, do you? Not I, my boy. I plan too far ahead for that. For the good of our cause it is my task to lose steadily and with good grace. This establishes my credit, proves my amiability, and confirms my popularity."

"But you are very much excited by something, Henriette," said I. "You cannot deny that."

"I don't—but it is the prospect of future gain, not the reality of present losses, that has taken me off my poise," she said. "Whom do you suppose I saw at Mrs. Gaster's to-day?"

"No detectives, I hope," I replied, paling at the thought.

"No, sir," she laughed. "Mrs. Gaster's maid. We must get her, Bunny."

"Oh, tush!" I ejaculated. "All this powwow over another woman's maid!"

"You don't understand," said Henriette. "It wasn't the maid so much as the woman that startled me, Bunny. You can't guess who she was."

"How should I?" I demanded.

"She was Fiametta de Belleville, one of the most expert hands in our business. Poor old Raffles used to say that she diminished his income a good ten thousand pounds a year by getting in her fine work ahead of his," explained Henriette. "He pointed her out to me in Piccadilly once and I have never forgotten her face."

"I hope she did not recognize you," I observed.

"No, indeed—she never saw me before, so how could she? But I knew her the minute she took my cloak," said Henriette. "She's dyed her hair, but her eyes were the same as ever, and that peculiar twist of the lip that Raffles had spoken of as constituting one of her fascinations remained unchanged.

Moreover, just to prove myself right, I left my lace handkerchief and a five hundred dollar bill in the cloak pocket. When I got the cloak back both were gone. Oh, she's Fiametta de Belleville all right, and we must get her."

"What for—to rob you?"

"No," returned Henrietta, "rather that we—but there, there, Bunny, I'll manage this little thing myself. It's a trifle too subtle for a man's intellect—especially when that man is you."

"What do you suppose she is doing here?" I asked.

"You silly boy," laughed Henriette.

"Doing? Why, Mrs. Gaster, of course. She is after the Gaster jewels."

"Humph!" I said, gloomily. "That cuts us out, doesn't it?"

"Does it?" asked Henriette, enigmatically.

It was about ten weeks later that the newspapers of the whole country were ringing with the startling news of the mysterious disappearance of Mrs. Gaster's jewels. The lady had been robbed of three hundred and sixty-eight thousand dollars worth of gems, and there was apparently no clew even to the thief. Henriette and I, of course, knew that Fiametta de Belleville had accomplished her mission, but apparently no one else knew it. True, she had been accused, and had been subjected to a most rigid examination by the Newport police and the New York Central Office, but no proof of any kind establishing her guilt could be adduced, and after a week of suspicion she was to all intents and purposes relieved of all odium.

"She'll skip now," said I.

"Not she," said Henriette. "To disappear now would be a confession of guilt. If Fiametta de Belleville is the woman I take her for she'll stay right here as if nothing had happened, but of course not at Mrs. Gaster's."

"Where then?" I asked.

"With Mrs. A. J. Van Raffles," replied Henriette. "The fact is," she added, "I have already engaged her. She has acted her part well, and has seemed so prostrated by the unjust suspicion of the world that even Mrs. Gaster is disturbed over her condition. She has asked her to remain, but Fiametta has refused. 'I couldn't, madam,' she said when Mrs. Gaster asked her to stay. 'You have accused me of a fearful crime—a crime of which I am innocent—and—I'd rather work in a factory, or become a shop-girl in a department store, than stay longer in a house where such painful things have happened.' Result, next Tuesday Fiametta de Belleville comes to me as *my* maid."

"Well, Henriette," said I, "I presume you know your own business, but why you lay yourself open to being robbed yourself and to having the profits of your own business diminished I can't see. Please remember that I warned you against this foolish act."

"All right, Bunny, I'll remember," smiled Mrs. Van Raffles, and there the matter was dropped for the moment.

The following Tuesday Fiametta de Belleville was installed in the Van Raffles household as the maid of Mrs. A. J. Van Raffles. To her eagle eye it was another promising field for profit, for Henriette had spared neither pains nor money to impress Fiametta with the idea that next to Mrs. Gaster she was about as lavish and financially capable a householder as could be found in the Social Capital of the United States. As for me, I was the picture of gloom. The woman's presence in our household could not be but a source of danger to our peace of mind as well as to our profits, and for the life of me I could not see why Henriette should want her there. But I was not long in finding out.

A week after Fiametta's arrival Mrs. Raffles rang hurriedly for me.

"Yes, madam," I said, responding immediately to her call.

"Bunny," she said, her hand trembling a little, "the hour for action has arrived. I have just sent Fiametta on an errand to Providence. She will be gone three hours."

"Yes!" said I. "What of it?"

"I want you during her absence to go with me to her room—"

The situation began to dawn on me.

"Yes!" I cried, breathlessly. "And search her trunks?"

"HER SLIGHT LITTLE FIGURE CONVULSED WITH GRIEF"

"No, Bunny, no—the eaves," whispered Henriette. "I gave her that room in the wing because it has so many odd cubby-holes where she could conceal things. I am inclined to think—well, the moment she leaves the city let me know. Follow her to the station, and don't return till you know she is safely out of town and on her way to Providence. Then *our* turn will come."

Oh, that woman! If I had not adored her before I—but enough. This is no place for sentiment. The story is the thing, and I must tell it briefly.

I followed out Henriette's instructions to the letter, and an hour later returned with the information that Fiametta was, indeed, safely on her way.

"Good," said Mrs. Raffles. "And now, Bunny, for the Gaster jewels."

Mounting the stairs rapidly, taking care, of course, that there were none of the other servants about to spy upon us, we came to the maid's room. Everything in it betokened a high mind and a good character. There were religious pictures upon the bureau, prayer-books, and some volumes of essays of a spiritual nature were scattered about—nothing was there to indicate that the occupant was anything but a simple, sweet child of innocence except—

Well, Henriette was right—except the Gaster jewels. Even as my mistress had suspected, they were cached under the eaves, snuggled close against the huge dormer-window looking out upon the gardens; laid by for a convenient moment to get them out of Newport, and then—back to England for Fiametta. And what a gorgeous collection they were! Dog-collars of diamonds, yards of pearl rope, necklaces of rubies of the most lustrous color and of the size of pigeons' eggs, rings, brooches, tiaras—everything in the way of jewelled ornament the soul of woman could desire—all packed closely away in a tin box that I now remembered Fiametta had brought with her in her hand the day of her arrival. And now all these things were ours—Henriette's and mine—without our having had to stir out-of-doors to get them. An hour later they were in the safety-deposit vault of Mrs. A. J. Van Raffles in the sturdy cellars of the Tiverton Trust Company, as secure against intrusion as though they were locked in the heart of Gibraltar itself.

And Fiametta? Well—a week later she left Newport suddenly, her eyes red with weeping and her slight little figure convulsed with grief. Her favorite aunt had just died, she said, and she was going back to England to bury her.

IV
THE PEARL ROPE OF MRS. GUSHINGTON-ANDREWS

"Bunny," said Henrietta one morning, shortly after we had come into possession of the Gaster jewels, "how is your nerve? Are you ready for a coup requiring a lot of it?"

"Well," I replied, pluming myself a bit, "I don't wish to boast, Henriette, but I think it is pretty good. I managed to raise twenty-seven hundred dollars on my own account by the use of it last night."

"Indeed?" said Henriette, with a slight frown. "How, Bunny? You know you are likely to complicate matters for all of us if you work on the side. What, pray, did you do last night?"

And then I unfolded to her the incidents of the night before when, by assuming at a moment's notice the position of valet to young Robertson de Pelt, the frisky young favorite of the inner set, I had relieved that high-flying young bachelor of fifteen hundred dollars in cash and some twelve hundred dollars worth of jewels as well.

"I was spending the evening at the Gentlemen's Gentlemen's Club," I explained, "when word came over the telephone to Digby, Mr. de Pelt's valet, that Mr. de Pelt was at the Rockerbilts' and in no condition to go home alone. It happened that it was I who took the message, and observing that Digby was engaged in a game of billiards, and likely to remain so for some time to come, I decided to go after the gentleman myself without saying anything to Digby about it. Muffling myself up so that no one could recognize me, I hired a cab and drove out to the Rockerbilt mansion, sent in word that Mr. de Pelt's man was waiting for him, and in ten minutes had the young gentleman in my possession. I took him to his apartment, dismissed the cab, and, letting ourselves into his room with his own latch-key, put him to bed. His clothes I took, as a well-ordered valet should, from his bed-chamber into an adjoining room, where, after removing the contents of his pockets, I hung them neatly over a chair and departed, taking with me, of course, everything of value the young gentleman had about him, even down to the two brilliant rubies he wore in his garter buckles. This consisted of two handfuls of crumpled twenty-dollar bills from his trousers, three rolls of one-hundred-dollar bills from his waistcoat, and sundry other lots of currency, both paper and specie, that I found stowed away in his overcoat and dinner-coat pockets. There were also ten twenty-dollar gold pieces in a little silver chain-bag he carried on his wrist. As I say, there was about fifteen hundred dollars of this loose change, and I reckon up the value of his studs, garter rubies, and finger-rings at about twelve hundred dollars more, or a twenty-seven hundred dollars pull in all. Eh?"

"Mercy, Bunny, that was a terribly risky thing. Suppose he had recognized you?" cried Henriette.

"Oh, he did—or at least he thought he did," I replied, smiling broadly at the recollection. "On the way home in the cab he wept on my shoulder and said I was the best friend he ever had, and told me he loved me like a brother. There wasn't anything he wouldn't do for me, and if ever I wanted an automobile or a grand-piano all I had to do was to ask him for it. He was very genial."

"Well, Bunny," said Henriette, "you are very clever at times, but do be careful. I am delighted to have you show your nerve now and then, but please don't take any serious chances. If Mr. de Pelt ever recognizes you—and he dines here next Wednesday—you'll get us both into awful trouble."

Again I laughed. "He won't," said I, with a conviction born of experience. "His geniality was of the kind that leaves the mind a blank the following morning. I don't believe Mr. de Pelt remembers now that he was at the Rockerbilts' last night, and even if he does, *you* know that I was in this house at eleven o'clock."

"I, Bunny? Why, I haven't seen you since dinner," she demurred.

"Nevertheless, Henriette, you know that I was in the house at eleven o'clock last night—or, rather, you *will* know it if you are ever questioned on the subject, which you won't be," said I. "So, now that I have shown you in just what shape my nerve is, what is the demand you are going to put upon it?"

"You will have to bring to the enterprise all that ability which used to characterize your efforts as an amateur actor, Bunny," she replied. "Summon all your sang-froid to your aid; act with deliberation, courtesy, and, above all, without the slightest manifestation of nervousness, and we should win, not a petty little twenty-seven hundred dollars, but as many thousands. You know Mrs. Gushington-Andrews?"

"Yes," said I. "She is the lady who asked me for the olives at your last dinner."

"Precisely," observed Henriette. "You possibly observed also that wherever she goes she wears about sixty-nine yards of pearl rope upon her person."

"Rope?" I laughed. "I shouldn't call that rope. Cable, yes—frankly, when she came into the dining-room the other night I thought it was a feather-boa she had on."

"All pearls, Bunny, of the finest water," said Henriette, enthusiastically. "There isn't one of the thousands that isn't worth anywhere from five hundred to twenty-five hundred."

"And I am to land a yard or two of the stuff for you in some mysterious way?" I demanded. "How is it to be—by kidnapping the lady, the snatch and run game, or how?"

"Sarcasm does not suit your complexion, Bunny," retorted Henriette. "Your best method is to follow implicitly the directions of wiser brains. You are a first-class tool, but as a principal—well—well, never mind. You do what I tell you and some of those pearls will be ours. Mrs. Gushington-Andrews, as you may have noticed, is one of those exceedingly effusive ladies who go into ecstasies over everything and everybody. She is what Raffles used to call a palaverer. Where most people nod she describes a complete circle with her head. When a cold, formal handshake is necessary she perpetrates an embrace, and that is where we come in. At my next Tuesday tea she will be present. She will wear her pearls—she'll be strung with them from head to foot. A rope-walk won't be in it with her, and every single little jewel will be worth a small fortune. You, Bunny, will be in the room to announce her when she arrives. She will rush to my arms, throw her own about my neck, the ornaments of my corsage will catch the rope at two or more points, sever the thread in several places, pearls will rain down upon the floor by dozens, and then—"

"I'm to snatch 'em and dive through the window, eh?" I interrupted.

"No, Bunny—you will behave like a gentleman, that is all," she responded, haughtily; "or rather like a butler with the instincts of a gentleman. At my cry of dismay over the accident—"

"Better call it the incident," I put in.

"Hush! At my cry of dismay over the accident," Henriette repeated, "you will spring forward, go down upon your knees, and gather up the jewels by the handful. You will pour them back into Mrs. Gushington-Andrews's hands and retire. Now, do you see?"

"H'm—yes," said I. "But how do you get the pearls if I pour them back into her hands? Am I to slide some of them under the rugs, or flick them with my thumb-nail under the piano—or what?"

"Nothing of the sort, Bunny; just do as I tell you—only bring your gloves to me just before the guests arrive, that is all," said Henriette. "Instinct will carry you through the rest of it."

And then the conspiracy stopped for the moment.

The following Tuesday at five the second of Mrs. Van Raffles's Tuesday afternoons began. Fortune favored us in that it was a beautiful day and the number of guests was large. Henriette was charming in her new gown specially imported from Paris—a gown of Oriental design with row upon row of brilliantly shining, crescent-shaped ornaments firmly affixed to the front of it and every one of them as sharp as a steel knife. I could see at a glance that even if so little as one of these fastened its talons upon the pearl rope of Mrs. Gushington-Andrews nothing under heaven could save it from laceration.

What a marvellous mind there lay behind those exquisite, childlike eyes of the wonderful Henriette!

"Remember, Bunny—calm deliberation—your gloves now," were her last words to me.

"Count on me, Henriette; but I still don't see—" I began.

"Hush! Just watch me," she replied.

Whereupon this wonderful creature, taking my white gloves, deliberately smeared their palms and inner sides of the fingers with a milk-hued paste of her own making, composed of talcum powder and liquid honey. Nothing more innocent-appearing yet more villainously sticky have I ever before encountered.

"There!" she said—and at last I understood.

An hour later our victim arrived and scarce an inch of her but shone like a snow-clad hill with the pearls she wore. I stood at the portière and announced Mrs. Gushington-Andrews in my most blasé but butlerian tones. The lady fairly rushed by me, and in a moment her arms were about Henriette's neck.

"You dear, sweet thing!" cried Mrs. Gushington-Andrews. "And you look so exquisitely charming to-day—"

"AND THEN THERE CAME A RIPPING SOUND"

And then there came a ripping sound. The two women started to draw away from each other; five of the crescents catching in the rope, in the impulsive jerking back of Mrs. Gushington-Andrews in order that she might gaze into Henrietta's eyes, cut through the marvellous cords of the exquisite jewels. There was a cry of dismay both from Henriette and her guest, and the rug beneath their feet was simply white with riches. In a moment I was upon my knees scooping them up by the handful.

"Oh, dear, how very unfortunate!" cried Henriette. "Here, dear," she added, holding out a pair of teacups. "Let James pour them into this," and James, otherwise myself, did so to the extent of five teacups full of them and then he discreetly retired.

"Well, Bunny," said Henriette, breathlessly, two hours later when her last guest had gone. "Tell me quickly—what was the result?"

"These, madam," said I, handing her a small plush bag into which I had poured the "salvage" taken from my sticky palms. "A good afternoon's work," I added.

And, egad, it was: seventeen pearls of a value of twelve hundred dollars each, fifteen worth scarcely less than nine hundred dollars apiece, and some twenty-seven or eight smaller ones that we held to be worth in the neighborhood of five hundred dollars each.

"Splendid!" cried Henrietta "Roughly speaking, Bunny, we've pulled in between forty and fifty thousand dollars to-day."

"I, OF COURSE, DID NOT TELL HENRIETTE OF EIGHT BEAUTIES I HAD KEPT OUT"

"About that," said I, with an inward chuckle, for I, of course, did not tell Henriette of eight beauties I had kept out of the returns for myself. "But what are we going to do when Mrs. Gushington-Andrews finds out that they are gone?"

"I shall provide for that," said this wonderful woman. "I shall throw her off the scent by sending you over to her at once with sixteen of these assorted. I hate to give them up, but I think it advisable to pay that much as a sort of insurance against suspicion. Even then we'll be thirty-five thousand dollars to the good. And, by-the-way, Bunny, I want to congratulate you on one thing."

"Ah! What's that—my sang-froid, my nerve?" I asked, airily.

"No, the size of your hands," said Henriette. "The superficial area of those palms of yours has been worth ten thousand dollars to us to-day."

V
THE ADVENTURE OF THE STEEL BONDS

"Excuse me, Henriette," said I one morning, after I had been in Mrs. Van Raffles's employ for about three months and had begun to calculate as to my share of the profits. "What are you doing with all this money we are gradually accumulating? There must be pretty near a million in hand by this time—eh?"

"One million two hundred and eighty-seven thousand five hundred and twenty-eight dollars and thirty-six cents," replied Henriette instantly. "It's a tidy little sum."

"Almost enough to retire on," I suggested.

"Now, Bunny, stop that!" retorted Henriette. "Either stop it or else retire yourself. I am not what they call a quitter in this country, and I do not propose at the very height of my career to give up a business which I have struggled for years to establish."

"That is all very well, Henriette," said I. "But the pitcher that goes to the bat too often strikes out at last." (I had become a baseball fiend during my sojourn in the States.) "A million dollars is a pot of money, and it's my advice to you to get away with it as soon as you can."

"Excuse me, Bunny, but when did I ever employ you to give advice?" demanded Henriette. "It is quite evident that you don't understand me. Do you suppose for an instant that I am robbing these people here in Newport merely for the vulgar purpose of acquiring money? If you do you have a woful misconception of the purposes which actuate an artist."

"You certainly are an artist, Henriette," I answered, desirous of placating her.

"Then you should know better than to intimate that I am in this business for the sordid dollars and cents there are to be got out of it," pouted my mistress. "Mr. Vauxhall Bean doesn't chase the aniseed bag because he loves to shed the aniseed or hungers for bags as an article of food. He does it for the excitement of the hunt; because he loves to feel the movement of the hunter that he sits so well between his knees; because he is enamoured of the baying of the hounds, the winding of the horn, and welcomes the element of personal danger that enters into the sport when he and his charger have to take an unusual fence or an extra broad watercourse. So with me. In separating these people here from their money and their jewels, it is not the money and the jewels that I care for so much as the delicious risks I incur in getting them. What the high fence is to the hunter, the barriers separating me from Mrs. Gaster's jewel-case are to me; what the watchful farmer armed with a shot-gun for the protection of his crops is to the master of the hounds, the police are to me. The game of circumventing the latter and surmounting the former are the joy of my life, and while my eyes flash and sparkle with appetite every time I see a necklace or a tiara or a roll of hundred-dollar bills in the course of my social duties, it is not avarice that makes them glitter, but the call to action which they sound."

I felt like saying that if that were the case I should esteem it a privilege to be made permanent custodian of the balance in hand, but it was quite evident from Henriette's manner that she was in no mood for badinage, so I held my peace.

"To prove to you that I am not out for the money, Bunny, I'll give you a check this morning for two hundred and fifty thousand dollars to pay you for those steel bonds you picked up on the train when you came up here from New York. That's two-and-a-half times what they are worth," said Henriette. "Is it a bargain?"

"Certainly, ma'am," I replied, delighted with the proposition. "But what are you going to do with the bonds?"

"Borrow a million and a half on 'em," said Henriette.

"What!" I cried. "A million and a half on a hundred thousand security?"

"Certainly," replied Henriette, "only it will require a little manipulation. For the past six months I have been depositing the moneys I have received in seventeen national banks in Ohio, each account being opened in a different name. The balances in each bank have averaged about three hundred thousand dollars, thanks to a circular system of checks in an endless chain that I have devised. Naturally the size of these accounts has hugely interested the bank officials, and they all regard me as a most desirable customer, and I think I can manage matters so that two or three of them, anyhow, will lend me all the money I want on those bonds and this certificate of trust which I shall ask you to sign."

"Me?" I laughed. "Surely you are joking. What value will my signature have?"

"It will be good as gold after you have deposited that check for two hundred and fifty thousand dollars in your New York bank," said Henriette. "I shall go to the president of the Ohoolihan National Bank at Oshkosh, Ohio, where I have at present three hundred and sixty-eight thousand three hundred and forty-three dollars and eighteen cents on deposit and tell him that the Hon. John Warrington Bunny, of New York, is my trustee for an estate of thirteen million dollars in funds set apart for me by a famous relative of mine who is not proud of the connection. He will communicate with you and ask you if this is true. You will respond by sending him a certified copy of the trust certificate, and refer him as to your own responsibility to the New York bank where our two hundred and fifty thousand dollars is on deposit. I will then swap checks with you for three hundred thousand dollars, mine to you going into your New York account and yours to me as trustee going into my account with the Ohoolihan National. The New York bank will naturally speak well of your balance, and the Ohoolihan people, finding the three-hundred-thousand-dollar check good, will never think of questioning your credit. This arranged, we will start in to wash those steel bonds up to the limit."

"That's a very simple little plan of yours, Henriette," said I, "and the first part of it will work easily I have no doubt; but how the deuce are you going to wash those bonds up to fifteen times their value?"

"Easiest thing in the world, Bunny," laughed Henriette. "There will be two million dollars of the bonds before I get through."

"Heavens—no counterfeiting, I hope?" I cried.

"Nothing so vulgar," said Henriette. "Just a little management—that's all. And, by-the-way, Bunny, when you get a chance, please hire twenty safe-deposit boxes for me in as many different trust companies here and in New York—and don't have 'em too near together. That's all for the present."

Three weeks later, having followed out Henriette's instructions to the letter, I received at my New York office a communication from the president of the Ohoolihan National Bank, of Oshkosh, Ohio, inquiring as to the Van Raffles trust fund. I replied with a certified copy of the original which Henriette had already placed in the president's hands. I incidentally referred the inquirer as to my own standing to the Delancy Trust Company, of New York. The three-hundred-thousand-dollar checks were exchanged by Henriette and myself—hers, by-the-way, was on the Seventy-Sixth National Bank, of Brookline, Massachusetts, and was signed by a fictitious male name, which shows how carefully she had covered her tracks. Both went through without question, and then the steel bonds came into play. Henriette applied for a loan of one million five hundred thousand dollars, offering the trust certificate for security. The president of the Ohoolihan National wished to see some of her other securities, if she had any, to which Henriette cordially replied that if he would come to New York she would gladly show them to him, and intimated that if the loan went through she wouldn't mind paying the bank a bonus of one hundred thousand dollars for the accommodation. The response was immediate. Mr. Bolivar would come on at once, and he did.

"'AFTER WHICH HE WILL COME TO NEWPORT'"

"Now, Bunny," said Mrs. Van Raffles on the morning of his arrival, "all you have to do is to put the one hundred bonds first in the vault of the Amalgamated Trust Company, of West Virginia, on Wall Street. Mr. Bolivar and I will go there and I will show them to him. We will then depart. Immediately after our departure you will get the bonds and take them to the vaults of the Trans-Missouri and Continental Trust Company, of New Jersey, on Broadway. You will go on foot, we in a hansom, so that you will get there first. I will take Mr. Bolivar in and show him the bonds again. Then you will take them to the vaults of the Riverside Coal Trust Company, of Pennsylvania, on Broad Street, where five minutes later I will show them for the third time to Mr. Bolivar—and so on. We will repeat this operation eighteen times in New York so that our visitor will fancy he has seen one million eight hundred thousand dollars' worth of bonds in all, after which he will come to Newport, where I will show them to him twice more—making a two-million-dollar show-down. See?"

I toppled back into a chair in sheer amazement.

"By Jingo! but you are a wonder," I cried. "If it only works."

"MR. BOLIVAR WAS DULY IMPRESSED WITH THE EXTENT OF HENRIETTE'S FORTUNE'"

It worked. Mr. Bolivar was duly impressed with the extent of Henriette's fortune in tangible assets, not to mention her evident standing in the community of her residence. He was charmingly entertained and never for an instant guessed when at dinner where Henriette had no less personages than the Rockerbilts, Mrs. Gaster, Mrs. Gushington-Andrews, Tommy Dare, and various other social lights to meet him, that the butler who passed him his soup and helped him liberally to wine was the Hon. John Warrington Bunny, trustee.

"Well," said Henriette, as she gazed delightedly at the president's certified check for one million four hundred thousand dollars—the amount of the loan less the bonus—"that was the best sport yet. Even aside from the size of the check, Bunny, it was great chasing the old man to cover. What do you think he said to me when he left, the poor, dear old innocent?"

"Give it up—what?"

"He said that I ought to be very careful in my dealings with men, who might impose upon my simplicity," laughed Henriette.

"Simplicity?" I roared. "What ever gave him the idea that you were simple?"

"Oh—I don't know," said Henriette, demurely. "I guess it was because I told him I kept those bonds in twenty safe-deposit vaults instead of in one, to protect myself in case of loss by fire—I didn't want to have too many eggs in one basket."

"H'm!" said I. "What did he say to that?"

Henriette laughed long and loud at the recollection of the aged bank president's reply.

"He squeezed my hand and answered, 'What a child it is, indeed!'" said Henriette.

VI
THE ADVENTURE OF THE FRESH-AIR FUND

It was a bright, sunny morning in the early summer when Henriette, gazing out of the dining-room windows across the lawns adjoining the Rockerbilt place, caught sight of a number of ragamuffins at play there.

"Who are those little tatterdemalions, Bunny?" she asked, with a suggestion of a frown upon her brow. "They have been playing on the lawns since seven o'clock this morning, and I've lost quite two hours' sleep because of their chatter."

"They are children from Mrs. Rockerbilt's Fresh-Air Society," I explained, for I, too, had been annoyed by the loud pranks of the youngsters and had made inquiries as to their identity. "Every summer, Digby, Mr. de Pelt's valet, tells me, Mrs. Rockerbilt gives a tea for the benefit of the Fresh-Air Fund, and she always has a dozen of the children from town for a week beforehand so as to get them in shape for the function."

"Get them in shape for the function, Bunny?" asked Henriette.

"Yes; one of the features of the tea is the presence of the youngsters, and they have to be pretty well rehearsed before Mrs. Rockerbilt dares let them loose among her guests," said I, for Digby had explained the scheme in detail to me. "You see, their ideas of fun are rather primitive, and if they were suddenly introduced into polite society without any previous training the results might prove unpleasant."

"Ah!" said Henriette, gazing abstractedly out of the window in the manner of one suddenly seized with an idea.

"Yes," I went on. "You see, the street gamin loves nothing better in the way of diversion than throwing things at somebody, particularly if that somebody is what is known to his vernacular as a Willie-boy. As between eating an over-ripe peach and throwing it at the pot-hat of a Willie-boy, the ragamuffin would deny even the cravings of his stomach for that tender morsel. It is his delight, too, to heave tin cans, wash-boilers, flat-irons, pies—anything he can lay his hands on—at the automobilly-boys, if I may use the term, of all of which, before he is turned loose in the highest social circles of the land, it is desirable that he shall be cured."

"I see," said Henriette. "And so Mrs. Rockerbilt has them here on a ten days' probation during which time they acquire that degree of savoir-faire and veneer of etiquette which alone makes it possible for her to exhibit them at her tea."

"Precisely," said I. "She lets them sleep in the big box-stalls of her stable where the extra coach-horses were kept before the motor-car craze came in. They receive four square meals a day, are rubbed down and curry-combed before each meal, and are bathed night and morning in violet water until the fateful occasion, after which they are returned to New York cleaner if not wiser children."

"It is a great charity," said Henrietta dreamily. "Does Mrs. Rockerbilt make any charge for admission to these teas—you say they are for the benefit of the Fresh-Air Fund?"

"Oh no, indeed," said I. "It is purely a private charity. The youngsters get their ten days in the country, learn good manners, and Newport society has a pleasant afternoon—all at Mrs. Rockerbilt's expense."

"H'm!" said Henriette, pensively. "H'm! I think there is a better method. Ah— I want you to run down to New York for a few days shortly, Bunny. I have a letter I wish you to mail."

Nothing more was said on the subject until the following Tuesday, when I was despatched to New York with instructions to organize myself into a Winter Fresh-Air Society, to have letter-heads printed, with the names of some of the most prominent ladies in society as patronesses—Henriette had secured permission from Mrs. Gaster, Mrs. Sloyd-Jinks, Mrs. Rockerbilt, Mrs. Gushington-Andrews, Mrs. R. U. Innitt, the duchess of Snarleyow, Mrs. Willie K. Van Pelt, and numerous others to use their names in connection with the new enterprise—and to write her a letter asking if she would not interest herself and her friends in the needs of the new society.

"It is quite as important," the letter ran, "that there should be a fund to take the little sufferers of our dreadful winters away from the sleet and snow-burdened streets of the freezing city as it is to give them their summer outing. This society is in great need of twenty-five thousand dollars properly to prosecute its work during the coming winter, and we appeal to you for aid."

Henriette's personal response to this request was a check for ten thousand dollars, which as secretary and treasurer of the fund I acknowledged, and then, of course, returned to her, whereupon her campaign began in earnest. Her own enthusiasm for the project, backed up by her most generous contribution, proved contagious, and inside of two weeks, not counting Henriette's check, we were in possession of over seventeen thousand dollars, one lady going so far as to give us all her bridge winnings for a week.

"And now for the grand coup, Bunny," said Mrs. Van Raffles, when I had returned with the spoil.

"Great Scot!" I cried. "Haven't you got enough?"

"No, Bunny. Not a quarter enough," she replied. "These winter resorts are very expensive places, and while seventeen thousand dollars would do very nicely for running a farm in summer, we shall need quite a hundred thousand to send our beneficiaries to Palm Beach in proper style."

"Phe-e-w!" I whistled, in amazement. "Palm Beach, eh?"

"Yes," said Henriette. "Palm Beach. I have always wanted to go there."

"And the one hundred thousand dollars—how do you propose to get that?" I demanded.

"I shall give a lawn-fête and bazaar for the benefit of the fund. It will differ from Mrs. Rockerbilt's tea in that I shall charge ten dollars admission, ten dollars to get out, and we shall sell things besides. I have already spoken to Mrs. Gaster about it and she is delighted with the idea. She has promised to stock the flower table with the cream of her conservatories. Mrs. Rockerbilt has volunteered to take charge of the refreshments. The duchess of Snarleyow is dressing a doll that is to be named by Senator Defew and raffled at five dollars a guess. Mrs. Gushington-Andrews is to take entire control of the fancy knick-knack table, where we shall sell gold match-boxes, solid silver automobile head-lights, cigar-cutters, cocktail-shakers, and other necessities of life among the select. I don't see how the thing can fail, do you?"

"Not so far," said I.

"Each of the twelve lady patronesses has promised to be responsible for the sale of a hundred tickets of admission at ten dollars apiece—that makes twelve thousand dollars in admissions. It will cost each person ten dollars more to get out, which, if only half of the tickets are used, will be six thousand dollars—or eighteen thousand dollars in entrance and exit fees alone."

"Henriette!" I cried, enthusiastically, "Madam Humbert was an amateur alongside of you."

Mrs. Van Raffles smiled. "Thank you, Bunny," said she. "If I'd only been a man—"

"Gad!" I ejaculated. "Wall Street would have been an infant in your hands."

Well, the fateful day came. Henriette, to do her justice, had herself spared no pains or expense to make the thing a success. I doubt if the gardens of the Constant-Scrappes ever looked so beautiful. There were flowers everywhere, and hanging from tree to tree from one end of their twenty acres to the other were long and graceful garlands of multicolored electric lights that when night came down upon the fête made the scene appear like a veritable glimpse of fairyland. Everybody that is anybody was there, with a multitude of others who may always be counted upon to pay well to see their names in print or to get a view of society at close range. Of course there was music of an entrancing sort, the numbers being especially designed to touch the flintiest of hearts, and Henriette was everywhere. No one, great or small, in that vast gathering but received one of her gracious smiles, and it is no exaggeration to say that half of the flowers purchased at rates that would make a Fifth Avenue tailor hang his head in shame, were bought by the gallant gentlemen of Newport for presentation to the hostess of the day. These were immediately placed on sale again so that on the flower account the receipts were perceptibly swelled.

A more festal occasion has never been known even in this festal environment. The richest of the land vied with one another in making the affair a vast financial success. The ever gallant Tommy Dare left the scene twenty times for the mere privilege of paying his way in and out that many times over at ten dollars each way. The doll which Senator Defew had named was also the cause of much merriment, since when all was over and some thirteen thousand five hundred dollars had been taken in for guesses, it was found that the senator had forgotten the name he had given it. When the laughter over this incident had subsided, Henriette suggested that it be put up at auction, which plan was immediately followed out, with the result that the handiwork of the duchess of Snarleyow was knocked down for eight thousand six hundred and seventy-five dollars to a Cincinnati brewer who had been trying for eight years to get his name into the Social Register.

"Thank goodness, that's over," said Henriette when the last guest had gone and the lights were out. "It has been a very delightful affair, but towards the end it began to get on my nerves. I am really appalled, Bunny, at the amount of money we have taken in."

"Did you get the full one hundred thousand dollars?" I asked.

"Full hundred thousand?" she cried, hysterically. "Listen to this." And she read the following memorandum of the day's receipts:

Flower Table	$36,000.00
Doll	22,175.00
Admissions	19,260.00
Exits	17,500.00
Candy Table	12,350.00
Supper Table	43,060.00

Knick-Knacks	17,380.00
Book Table	123.30
Coat Checks	3,340.00
Total	$171,188.30

"Great Heavens, what a haul!" I cried. "But how much did you spend yourself?"

"Oh—about twenty thousand dollars, Bunny—I really felt I could afford it. We'll net not less than one hundred and fifty thousand."

I was suddenly seized with a chill.

"The thing scares me, Henriette," I murmured. "Suppose these people ask you next winter for a report?"

"Oh," laughed Henriette, "I shall immediately turn the money over to the fund. You can send me a receipt and that will let us out. Later on you can return the money to me."

"Even then—" I began.

"Tush, Bunny," said she. "There isn't going to be any even then. Six months from now these people will have forgotten all about it. It's a little way they have. Their memory for faces and the money they spend is shorter than the purse of a bankrupt. Have no fear."

And, as usual, Henriette was right, for the next February when the beneficiaries of the Winter Fresh-Air Fund spent a month at Palm Beach, enjoying the best that favored spot afforded in the way of entertainment and diversion, not a word of criticism was advanced by anybody, although the party consisted solely of Mrs. Van Raffles, her maid, and Bunny, her butler. In fact, the contrary was the truth. The people we met while there, many of whom had contributed most largely to the fund, welcomed us with open arms, little suspecting how intimately connected they were with our sources of supply.

Mrs. Gaster, it is true, did ask Henriette how the Winter Fresh-Air Fund was doing and was told the truth—that it was doing very well.

"The beneficiaries did very well here," said Henriette.

"I have seen nothing of them," observed Mrs. Gaster.

"Well—no," said Henriette. "The managers thought it was better to send them here before the season was at its height. The moral influences of Palm Beach at the top of the season are—well—a trifle strong for the young—don't you think?" she explained.

The tin-type I hand you will give you some idea of how much one of the beneficiaries enjoyed himself. There is nothing finer in the world than surf bathing in winter.

ONE OF THE BENEFICIARIES AT PALM BEACH
(From a tin-type taken on the spot)

VII
THE ADVENTURE OF MRS. ROCKERBILT'S TIARA

Henriette had been unwontedly reserved for a whole week, a fact which was beginning to get sadly on my nerves when she broke an almost Sphinxlike silence with the extraordinary remark:

"Bunny, I am sorry, but I don't see any other way out of it. You must get married."

To say that I was shocked by the observation is putting it mildly. As you must by this time have realized yourself, there was only one woman in the world that I could possibly bring myself to think fondly of, and that woman was none other than Henriette herself. I could not believe, however, that this was at all the notion she had in mind, and what little poise I had was completely shattered by the suggestion.

I drew myself up with dignity, however, in a moment and answered her.

"Very well, dear," I said. "Whenever you are ready I am. You must have banked enough by this time to be able to support me in the style to which I am accustomed."

"That is not what I meant, Bunny," she retorted, coldly, frowning at me.

"Well, it's what *I* mean," said I. "You are the only woman I ever loved—"

"But, Bunny dear, that can come later," said she, with a charming little blush. "What I meant, my dear boy, was not a permanent affair but one of these Newport marriages. Not necessarily for publication, but as a guarantee of good faith," she explained.

"I don't understand," said I, affecting denseness, for I understood only too well.

"Stupid!" cried Henriette. "I need a confidential maid, Bunny, to help us in our business, and I don't want to take a third party in at random. If you had a wife I could trust her. You could stay married as long as we needed her, and then, following the Newport plan, you could get rid of her and marry me later—that is—er—provided I was willing to marry you at all, and I am not so sure that I shall not be some day, when I am old and toothless."

"I fail to see the necessity for a maid of that kind," said I.

"That's because you are a man, Bunny," said Henriette. "There are splendid opportunities for acquiring the gems these Newport ladies wear by one who may be stationed in the dressing-room. There is Mrs. Rockerbilt's tiara, for instance. It is at present the finest thing of its kind in existence and of priceless value. When she isn't wearing it it is kept in the vaults of the Tiverton Trust Company, and how on earth we are to get it without the assistance of a maid we can trust I don't see—except in the vulgar, commonplace way of sandbagging the lady and brutally stealing it, and Newport society hasn't quite got to the point where you can do a thing like that to a woman without causing talk, unless you are married to her."

"Well, I'll tell you one thing, Henriette," I returned, with more positiveness than I commonly show, "I will not marry a lady's maid, and that's all there is about it. You forget that I am a gentleman."

"It's only a temporary arrangement, Bunny," she pleaded. "It's done all the time in the smart set."

"Well, the morals of the smart set are not my morals," I retorted. "My father was a clergyman, Henriette, and I'm something of a churchman myself, and I won't stoop to such baseness. Besides, what's to prevent my wife from blabbing when we try to ship her?"

"H'm!" mused Henriette. "I hadn't thought of that—it would be dangerous, wouldn't it?"

"Very," said I. "The only safe way out of it would be to kill the young woman, and my religious scruples are strongly against anything of the sort. You must remember, Henriette, that there are one or two of the commandments that I hold in too high esteem to break them."

"Then what shall we do, Bunny?" demanded Mrs. Van Raffles. "*I must have that tiara.*"

"Well, there's the old amateur theatrical method," said I. "Have a little play here, reproduce Mrs. Rockerbilt's tiara in paste for one of the characters to wear, substitute the spurious for the real, and there you are."

"That is a good idea," said Henriette; "only I hate amateur theatricals. I'll think it over."

A few days later my mistress summoned me again.

"Bunny, you used to make fairly good sketches, didn't you?" she asked.

"Pretty good," said I. "Chiefly architectural drawings, however—details of façades and ornamental designs."

"Just the thing!" cried Henriette. "To-night Mrs. Rockerbilt gives a moonlight reception on her lawns. They adjoin ours. She will wear her tiara, and I want you when she is in the gardens to hide behind some convenient bit of shrubbery and make an exact detail sketch of the tiara. Understand?"

"I do," said I.

"Don't you miss a ruby or a diamond or the teeniest bit of filigree, Bunny. Get the whole thing to a carat," she commanded.

"And then?" I asked, excitedly.

"Bring it to me; I'll attend to the rest," said she.

"IT WAS NOT ALWAYS EASY TO GET THE RIGHT LIGHT"

You may be sure that when night came I went at the work in hand with alacrity. It was not always easy to get the right light on the lady's tiara, but in several different quarters of the garden I got her sufficiently well, though unconsciously, posed to accomplish my purpose. Once I nearly yielded to the temptation to reach my hand through the shrubbery and snatch the superb ornament from Mrs. Rockerbilt's head, for she was quite close enough to make this possible, but the vulgarity of such an operation was so very evident that I put it aside almost as soon as thought of. And I have always remembered dear old Raffles's remark, "Take everything in sight, Bunny," he used to say; "but, damn it, do it like a gentleman, not a professional."

The sketch made, I took it to my room and colored it, so that that night, when Henriette returned, I had ready for her a perfect pictorial representation of the much-coveted bauble.

"It is simply perfect, Bunny," she cried, delightedly, as she looked at it. "You have even got the sparkle of that incomparable ruby in the front."

Next morning we went to New York, and Henriette, taking my design to a theatrical property-man we knew on Union Square, left an order for its exact reproduction in gilt and paste.

"I am going to a little fancy-dress dance, Mr. Sikes," she explained, "as Queen Catharine of Russia, and this tiara is a copy of the very famous lost negligée crown of that unhappy queen. Do you think you can let me have it by Tuesday next?"

"Easily, madam," said Sikes. "It is a beautiful thing and it will give me real pleasure to reproduce it. I'll guarantee it will be so like the original that the queen herself couldn't tell 'em apart. It will cost you forty-eight dollars.

"Agreed," said Henriette.

And Sikes was true to his word. The following Tuesday afternoon brought to my New York apartment—for of course Mrs. Raffles did not give Sikes her right name—an absolutely faultless copy of Mrs. Rockerbilt's chiefest glory. It was so like that none but an expert in gems could have told the copy from the original, and when I bore the package back to Newport and displayed its contents to my mistress she flew into an ecstasy of delight.

"We'll have the original in a week if you keep your nerve, Bunny," she cried.

"Theatricals?" said I.

"No, indeed," said Henriette. "If Mrs. Rockerbilt knew this copy was in existence she'd never wear the other in public again as long as she lived without bringing a dozen detectives along with her. No, indeed—a dinner. I want you to connect the electric lights of the dining-room with the push-button at my foot, so that at any moment I can throw the dining-room into darkness. Mrs. Rockerbilt will sit at my left—Tommy Dare to the right. She will wear her famous coiffure surmounted by the tiara. At the moment you are passing the poisson I will throw the room into darkness, and you—"

"I positively decline, Henriette, to substitute one tiara for another in the dark. Why, darn it all, she'd scream the minute I tried it," I protested.

"Of course she would," said she, impatiently. "And that is why I don't propose any such idiotic performance. You will merely stumble in the dark and manage your elbow so awkwardly that Mrs. Rockerbilt's coiffure will be entirely disarranged by it. She will scream, of course, and I will instantly restore the light, after which I will attend to the substitution. Now don't fail me and the tiara will be ours."

"ALL WAS AS HENRIETTE HAD FORETOLD"

I stand ready with affidavits to prove that that dinner was the most exciting affair of my life. At one time it seemed to me that I could not possibly perform my share of the conspiracy without detection, but a glance at Henriette, sitting calmly and coolly, and beautiful too, by gad, at the head of the table, chatting as affably with the duke of Snarleyow and Tommy Dare as though there was nothing in the wind, nerved me to action. The moment came, and instantly as I leaned over Mrs. Rockerbilt's side with the fish platter in my hand out went the light; crash went my elbow into the lady's stunning coiffure; her little, well-modulated scream of surprise rent the air, and, flash, back came the lights again. All was as Henriette had foretold, Mrs. Rockerbilt's lovely blond locks were frightfully demoralized, and the famous tiara with it had slid aslant athwart her cheek.

"Dear me!" cried Henriette, rising hurriedly and full of warm sympathy. "How very awkward!"

"Oh, don't speak of it," laughed Mrs. Rockerbilt, amiably. "It is nothing, dear Mrs. Van Raffles. These electric lights are so very uncertain these days, and I am sure James is not at all to blame for hitting me as he has done; it's the most natural thing in the world, only—may I please run up-stairs and fix my hair again?"

"You most certainly shall," said Henriette. "And I will go with you, my dear Emily. I am so mortified that if you will let me do penance in that way I will myself restore order out of this lovely chaos."

The little speech was received with the usual hilarious appreciation which follows anything out of the usual course of events in high social circles. Tommy Dare gave three cheers for Mrs. Van Raffles, and Mrs. Gramercy Van Pelt, clad in a gorgeous red costume, stood up on a chair and toasted me in a bumper of champagne. Meanwhile Henriette and Mrs. Rockerbilt had gone above.

"Isn't it a beauty, Bunny," said Henriette the next morning, as she held up the tiara to my admiring gaze, a flashing, coruscating bit of the jeweler's art that, I verily believe, would have tempted the soul of honor itself into rascally ways.

"Magnificent!" I asserted. "But—which is this, the forty-eight-dollar one or the original?"

"The original," said Henriette, caressing the bauble. "You see, when we got to my room last night and I had Mrs. Rockerbilt sitting before the mirror, and despite her protestations was fixing her dishevelled locks with my own fair hands, I arranged to have the lights go out again just as the tiara was laid on the dressing-table. The copy was in the table drawer, and while my right hand was apparently engaged in manipulating the refractory light, and my voice was laughingly calling down maledictions upon the electric lighting company for its wretched service, my left hand was occupied with the busiest effort of its career in substituting the spurious tiara for the other."

"And Mrs. Rockerbilt never even suspected?"

"No," said Henriette. "In fact, she placed the bogus affair in her hair herself. As far as her knowledge goes, I never even touched the original."

"Well, you're a wonder, Henriette," said I, with a sigh. "Still, if Mrs. Rockerbilt should ever discover—"

"She won't, Bunny," said Henriette. "She'll never have occasion to test the genuineness of her tiara. These Newport people have other sources of income than the vulgar pawnshops."

But, alas! later on Henriette made a discovery herself that for the time being turned her eyes red with weeping. The Rockerbilt tiara itself was as bogus as our own copy. There wasn't a real stone in the whole outfit, and the worst part of it was that under the circumstances Henriette could not tell anybody over the teacups that Mrs. Rockerbilt was, in vulgar parlance, "putting up a shine" on high society.

VIII
THE ADVENTURE OF THE CARNEGIE LIBRARY

"Merciful Midas, Bunny," said Henriette one morning as I was removing the breakfast-tray from her apartment. "Did you see the extent of Mr. Carnegie's benefactions in the published list this morning?"

"I have not received my paper yet," said I. "Moreover, I doubt if it will contain any reference to such matters when it does come. You know I read only the London *Times*, Mrs. Van Raffles. I haven't been able to go the American newspapers."

"More fool you, then, Bunny," laughed my mistress. "Any man who wants to pursue crime as a polite diversion and does not read the American newspapers fails to avail himself of one of the most potent instruments for the attainment of the highest artistic results. You cannot pick up a newspaper in any part of the land without discovering somewhere in its columns some reference to a new variety of house-breaking, some new and highly artistic method of writing another man's autograph so that when appended to a check and presented at his bank it will bear the closest scrutiny to which the paying-teller will subject it, some truly Napoleonic method of entirely novel design for the sudden parting of the rich from their possessions. Any university which attempted to add a School of Peculation to its curriculum and ignored the daily papers as a positive source of inspiration to the highest artistry in the profession would fail as ignobly as though it should forget to teach the fundamental principles of high finance."

"I was not aware of their proficiency in that direction," said I.

"You never will get on, Bunny," sighed Henriette, "because you are not quick to seize opportunities that lie directly under your nose. How do you suppose I first learned of all this graft at Newport? Why, by reading the newspaper accounts of their jewels in the Sunday and daily newspapers. How do I know that if I want to sand-bag Mr. Rockerbilt and rifle his pockets all I have to do is to station myself outside the Crackerbaker Club any dark opera night after twelve and catch him on his way home with his fortune sticking out all over him? Because the newspapers tell me that he is a regular habitué of the Crackerbaker and plays bridge there every night after the opera. How do I know just how to walk from my hall bedroom in my little East Side tenement up Fifth Avenue into Mrs. Gaster's dining-room, where she has a million in plate on her buffet, with my eyes shut, without fear of stumbling over a step or a chair or even a footstool? Because the newspapers have so repeatedly printed diagrams of the interior of the lady's residence that its halls, passages, doorways, exits, twists, turns, and culs-de-sac are indelibly engraved upon my mind. How did I acquire my wonderful knowledge of the exact number of pearls, rubies, diamonds, opals, tiaras, bracelets, necklaces, stomachers, and other gorgeous jewels now in the possession of the smart set? Only by an assiduous devotion to the contents of the daily newspapers in their reports of the doings of the socially elect. I have a scrap-book, Bunny, that has been two years in the making, and there hasn't been a novel burglary reported in all that time that is not recorded in my book, not a gem that has appeared at the opera, the theatre, the Charity Ball, the Horse Show, or a monkey dinner that has not been duly noted in this vademecum of mine, fully described and in a sense located. If it wasn't for that knowledge I could not hope for success any more than you could if you went hunting mountain-lions in the Desert of Sahara, or tried to lure speckled-trout from the depths of an empty goldfish globe."

"I see," said I, meekly. "I have missed a great opportunity. I will subscribe to the *Tribune* and *Evening Post* right away."

I have never understood why Henriette greeted this observation with a peal of silvery laughter that fairly made the welkin ring. All I know is that it so irritated me that I left the room to keep from making a retort that might seriously have disturbed our friendship. Later in the day, Mrs. Van Raffles rang for me and I attended upon her orders.

"Bunny," said she, "I've made up my mind to it—I must have a Carnegie library, that is all there is about it, and you must help. The iron-master has already spent thirty-nine million dollars on that sort of thing, and I don't see why if other people can get 'em we can't."

"Possibly because we are not a city, town, or hamlet," I suggested, for I had been looking over the daily papers since my morning's talk with the lady, and had observed just who had been the beneficiaries of Mr. Carnegie's benefactions. "He don't give 'em to individuals, but to communities."

"Of course not," she responded, quickly. "But what is to prevent our becoming a municipality?"

My answer was an amazed silence, for frankly I could not for the life of me guess how we were to do any such thing.

"It's the easiest thing in the world," she continued. "All you have to do is to buy an abandoned farm on Long Island with a bleak sea-front, divide it up into corner lots, advertise the lots for sale on the instalment plan, elect your mayor, and Raffleshurst-by-the-Sea, swept by ocean breezes, fifteen cents from the Battery, is a living, breathing reality."

"By the jumping Disraeli, Henriette, but you are a marvel!" I cried, with enthusiasm. "But," I added, my ardor cooling a little, "won't it cost money?"

"About fifteen hundred dollars," said Henriette. "I can win that at bridge in an hour."

"Well," said I, "you know you can command my services, Henriette. What shall I do?"

"Organize the city," she replied. "Here is fifty dollars. That will do for a starter. Go down to Long Island, buy the farm, put up a few signs calling on people to own their own homes; advertise the place in big capital letters in the Sunday papers as likely to be the port of the future, consider yourself duly elected mayor, stop in at some photograph shop in New York on your way back and get a few dozen pictures of street scenes in Binghamton, Oberlin, Kalamazoo, and other well-populated cities, and then come back here for further instructions. Meanwhile I will work out the other details of the scheme."

According to my habit I followed Henriette's instructions to the letter. A farm of five hundred acres was secured within a week, the bleakest, coldest spot ever swept by ocean breezes anywhere. It cost six hundred dollars in cash, with immediate possession. Three days later, with the use of a ruler, I had mapped out about twelve thousand corner lots on the thing, and, thanks to my knack at draughtsmanship, had all ready for anybody's inspection as fine a ground-plan of Raffleshurst-by-the-Sea as ever was got up by a land-booming company in this or any other country. I then secured the photographs desired by my mistress, advertised Raffleshurst in three Sunday newspapers to the tune of a half-page each, and returned to Newport. I flattered myself that the thing was well done, for on reading the advertisement nothing would do but that Henriette should visit the place in person. The ads were so phrased, she said, as to be irresistible.

"It's fine, Bunny," she cried, with an enthusiastic laugh as she gazed out over the broad acres of Raffleshurst and noted how well I had fulfilled her orders. "Under proper direction you are a most able workman. Nothing could be better. Nothing—absolutely nothing. And now for Mr. Carnegie."

I still did not see how the thing was coming out, but such was my confidence in my leader that I had no misgivings.

"Here is a letter from Mrs. Gaster introducing the Hon. Henry Higginbotham, mayor of Raffleshurst, to Mr. Carnegie," said Henriette. "You will call at once on the iron-master. Present this letter, keeping in mind of course that you are yourself the Hon. Henry Higginbotham. Show him these photographs of the City Hall at Binghamton, of the public park at Oberlin, the high school at Oswego, the battery walk at Charleston and other public improvements of various other cities, when he asks you what sort of a place Raffleshurst is; then frankly and fearlessly put in your application for a one-hundred-and-fifty-thousand-dollar library. One picture—this beautiful photograph of the music-hall at the St. Louis Exhibition—you must seem to overlook always, only contrive matters so that he will inquire what it is. You must then modestly remark that it is nothing but a little two-hundred-thousand-dollar art gallery you have yourself presented to the town. See?"

"H'm—yes, I see," said I. "But it is pretty risky business, Henriette. Suppose Mrs. Gaster asks for further information about Mayor Higginbotham? I think it was unwise of you to connect her with the enterprise."

"Don't bother about that, Bunny. *I* wrote that letter of introduction—I haven't studied penmanship for nothing, you know. Mrs. Gaster will never know. So just put on your boldest front, remember your name, and don't forget to be modest about your own two-hundred-thousand-dollar art gallery. That will inspire him, I think."

It took me a week to get at the iron-master; but finally, thanks to Mrs. Gaster's letter of introduction, I succeeded. Mr. Carnegie was as always in a most amiable frame of mind, and received me cordially, even when he discovered my real business with him.

"'IF YOU WANTED A LAKE, MR. HIGGINBOTHAM, I—'"

"I hadn't intended to give any more libraries this year," he said, as he glanced over the pictures. "I am giving away lakes now," he added. "If you wanted a lake, Mr. Higginbotham, I—"

"We have such a large water-front already, Mr. Carnegie," said I, "and most of our residents are young married couples with children not over three and five. I am afraid they would regard a lake as a source of danger."

"That's a pretty playground," he suggested, glancing at the Oberlin Park. "Somehow or other, it reminds me of something."

I thought it quite likely, but, of course, I didn't say so. I may be a fool but I have some tact.

"It's at the far corner of the park that we propose to put the library if you are good enough to let us have it," was all I ventured.

"H'm!" he mused. "Well, do you know, I like to help people who help themselves—that's my system."

I assured him that we of Raffleshurst were accustomed to helping ourselves to everything we could lay our hands on, a jest which even though it was only too true seemed to strike him pleasantly.

"What is that handsome structure you always pass over?" he asked, as I contrived to push the music-hall photograph aside for the fifth time.

I laughed deprecatingly. "Oh, that," I said, modestly—"that's only a little two-hundred-thousand-dollar music-hall and art gallery I have built for the town myself."

Oh, that wonderful Henriette! How did she know that generosity even among the overgenerous was infectious?

"Indeed!" said Mr. Carnegie, his face lighting up with real pleasure. "Well, Mr. Higginbotham, I guess— I guess I'll do it. I can't be outdone in generosity by you, sir, and—er— I guess you can count on the library. Do you think one hundred and fifty thousand dollars will be enough?"

"Well, of course—" I began.

"Why not make my contribution equal to yours and call it an even two hundred thousand dollars?" he interrupted.

"You overwhelm me," said I. "Of course, if you wish to—"

"And the Raffleshurst common council will appropriate five per cent. of that amount annually for its maintenance?" he inquired.

"Such a resolution has already been passed," said I, taking a paper from my pocket. "Here is the ordinance, duly signed by myself as mayor and by the secretary of the council."

Again that extraordinary woman, to provide me with so necessary a document!

The millionaire rose with alacrity and with his own hand drew me the required check.

"Mr. Mayor," said he, "I like the quick, business-like way in which you do things. Pray present my compliments to the citizens of Raffleshurst-by-the-Sea, and tell them I am only too glad to help them. If you ever want a lake, sir, don't fail to call upon me." With which gracious words the millionaire bowed me out.

"*Two* hundred thousand dollars, Bunny?" cried Henriette when I handed her the check.

"Yep," said I.

"Well, that *is* a good day's sport!" she said, gazing at the slip. "Twice as much as I expected."

"Yes," said I. "But see here, Henrietta, suppose Mr. Carnegie should go down to Raffleshurst to see the new building and find out what a bunco game we have played on him?"

"He's not likely to do that for two reasons, Bunny," she replied. "In the first place he suffers acutely from lumbago in winter and can't travel, and in the second place he'd have to find Raffleshurst-by-the-Sea before he could make the discovery that somebody'd put up a game on him. I think by the time he is ready to start we can arrange matters to have Raffleshurst taken off the map."

"Well, I think this is the cleverest trick you've turned yet, Henriette," said I.

"Nonsense, Bunny, nonsense," she replied. "Any idiot can get a Carnegie library these days. That's why I put *you* on the job, dear," she added, affectionately.

IX
THE ADVENTURE OF THE HOLD-UP

Now that it is all over, I do not know whether she was really worn-out or by the expert use of powder gave to her cheeks the pallid look which bore out Mrs. Van Raffles's statement to me that she needed a rest. At any rate, one morning in mid-August, when the Newport season was in full feather, Henriette, looking very pale and wan, tearfully confessed to me that business had got on her nerves and that she was going away to a rest-cure on the Hudson for ten days.

"I just can't stand it for another minute, Bunny," she faltered, real tears coursing down her cheeks. "I haven't slept a wink of natural sleep for five days, and yet when night comes it is all I can do to keep my eyes open. At the Rockerbilt ball last night I dozed off four times while talking with the Duchess of Snarleyow, and when the Chinese Ambassador asked me to sit out the gavotte with him I'm told I actually snored in his face. A woman who can't keep awake all night and sleep properly by day is not fit for Newport society, and I've simply got to go away and get my nerve back again."

"You are very wise," I replied, "and I wholly approve of your course. There is no use of trying to do too much and you have begun to show the strain to which you have been subjecting yourself. Your failure last Friday night to land Mrs. Gollet's ruby dog-collar when her French poodle sat in your lap all through the Gaster musicale is evidence to me that your mind is not as alert as usual. By all means, go away and rest up. I'll take care of things around here."

"Thank you, dear," said she, with a grateful smile. "You need a change too, Bunny. What would you say if I sent all the servants away too, so that you could have a week of absolute tranquillity? It must be awful for a man of your refined sensibilities to have to associate so constantly with the housemaids, the under-butlers and the footmen."

"Nothing would please me better," I returned with alacrity; for, to tell the truth, society below stairs was rapidly becoming caviar to my taste. The housemaids were all right, and the under-butlers, being properly subject to my control, I could wither when they grew too familiar, but the footmen were intolerable guyers. On more than one occasion their quick Irish wit had put me to my trumps to maintain my dignity, and I had noticed of late that their alleged fun at my expense had made even the parlormaid giggle in a most irritating fashion. Henriette's suggestion promised at least a week's immunity from this sort of thing, and as far as remaining alone in the beautiful Bolivar Lodge was concerned, to a man of my literary and artistic tastes nothing could be more desirable.

"I can put in a week of solitude here very comfortably," said I. "The Constant-Scrappes have a very excellent library and a line of reading in Abstract Morals in full calf that I should very much like to get at."

"So be it then," said Henriette, with a sigh of relief. "I will take my departure next Saturday after the Innitt's clam-bake on Honk Island. The servants can go Saturday afternoon after the house has been put in order. You can order a fresh supply of champagne and cigars for yourself, and as for your meals—"

"Don't you bother about that," said I, with a laugh. "I lived for months on the chafing-dish before I found you again. And I rather think the change from game birds and pâté de foie gras to simple eggs and bread and butter will do me good."

And so the matter was arranged. The servants were notified that, owing to Mrs. Van Raffles's illness, they might take a vacation on full pay for ten days, and Henriette herself prepared society for her departure by fainting twice at the Innit's clam-bake on Honk Island.

No less a person than Mrs. Gaster herself brought her home at four o'clock in the morning and her last words were an exhortation to her "*dear* Mrs. Van Raffles" to be careful of herself "for all our sakes." Saturday morning Henriette departed. Saturday afternoon the servants followed suit, and I was alone in my glory—and oh, how I revelled in it! The beauties of Bolivar Lodge had never so revealed themselves to me as then; the house as dark as the tomb without, thanks to the closing of the shutters and the drawing to of all the heavy portières before the windows, but a blaze of light within from cellar to roof. I spent whole hours gloating over the treasures of that Monte-Cristan treasure-house, and all day Sunday and Monday I spent poring over the books in the library, a marvellous collection, though for the most part wholly uncut.

Everything moved along serenely until Wednesday afternoon, when I thought I heard a noise in the cellar, but investigation revealed the presence of no one but a stray cat which miaowed up the cellar steps to me in response to my call of "Who's there." True, I did not go down to see if any one were there, not caring to involve myself in a personal encounter with a chance tramp who might have wandered in, in search of food. The sudden materialization of the cat satisfactorily explained the noises, and I returned to the library to resume my reading of *The Origin of the Decalogue* where I had left off at the moment of the interruption. That evening I cooked myself a welsh-rabbit and at eight o'clock, arrayed in my pajamas, I returned to the library with a book, a bottle of champagne and a box of Vencedoras, prepared for a quiet evening of absolute luxury. I read in the waning light of the dying midsummer day for a little while, and then, as darkness came on, I turned to the switch-board to light the electric lamp.

The lamp would not light.

I pressed and pressed every button in the room, but with no better results; and then, going through the house I tried every other button I could find, but everywhere conditions were the same. Apparently there was something the matter with the electrical service, a fact which I cursed, but not deeply, for it was a beautiful moonlight night and while of course I was disappointed in my reading, I realized that after all nothing could be pleasanter than to sit in the moonlight and smoke and quaff bumpers of champagne until the crack of doom. This I immediately proceeded to do, and kept at it pretty steadily until I should say about eleven o'clock, when I heard unmistakable signs of a large automobile coming up the drive. It chugged as far as the front-door and then stood panting like an impatient steam-engine, while the chauffeur, a person of medium height, well muffled in his automobile coat, his features concealed behind his goggles, and his mouth covered by his collar, rapped loudly on the front-door, once, then a second time.

"Who the devil can this be at this hour of the night, I wonder," I muttered, as I responded to the summons.

If I sought the name I was not to be gratified, for the moment I opened the door I found two pistols levelled upon me, and two very determined eyes peering at me from behind the goggles.

"Not a word, or I shoot," said the intruder in a gruff voice, evidently assumed, before I could get a word from my already somewhat champagne-twisted tongue. "Lead me to the dining-room."

Well, there I was. Defenceless, taken by surprise, unarmed, not too wide awake, comfortably filled with champagne and in no particularly fighting mood. What could I do but yield? To call for help would have brought at least two bullets crashing into my brain, even if any one could have heard my cries. To assault a scoundrel so well-armed would have been the height of folly, and to tell the truth so imbued was I with the politer spirit of the gentle art of house-breaking that this sudden confrontation with the ruder, rough-house methods of the highwayman left me entirely unable to cope with the situation.

"Certainly," said I, turning and ushering him down the hall to the great dining-room where the marvellous plate of the Constant-Scrappes shone effulgently upon the sideboard—or at least such of it as there was no room for in the massive safe.

"Get me some rope," commanded the intruder. Still under the range of those dreadful pistols, I obeyed.

"Sit down in that chair, and, by the leaping Gladstone, if you move an inch I'll blow your face off feature by feature," growled the intruder.

"Who's moving?" I retorted, angrily.

"Well, see that whoever else is you are not," he retorted, winding the rope three times around my waist and fastening me securely to the back of the chair. "Now hold out your hands."

I obeyed, and he bound them as tightly as though they were fastened together with rods of iron. A moment later my feet and knees were similarly bound and I was as fast in the toils as Gulliver, when the Liliputians fell upon him in his sleep and bound him to the earth.

"AS KEEN AND HIGH-HANDED A PERFORMANCE AS I EVER WITNESSED"

And then I was a mute witness to as keen and high-handed a performance as I ever witnessed. One by one every item of the Constant-Scrappe's silver service, valued at ninety thousand dollars, was removed from the sideboard and taken along the hall and placed in the tonneau of the automobile. Next the safe in which lay not only the famous gold service used only at the very swellest functions, said to have cost one hundred and seventy-five thousand dollars for the gold alone, to say nothing of the exquisite workmanship, but—it made me gnash my teeth in impotent rage to see it—Henriette's own jewel-box containing a hundred thousand dollars worth of her own gems and some thirty thousand dollars in cash, was rifled of its contents and disposed of similarly to the silver in the gaping maw of that damned automobile tonneau.

"Now," said the intruder, loosening my feet and releasing me from the chair, "take me to my lady's boudoir. There is room in the car for a few more objects of virtu."

I obeyed on the instant and a few moments later the scene of below-stairs was repeated, with me powerless to resist. Pictures, bric-à-brac, and other things to the tune of twenty thousand dollars more were removed, as calmly and as coolly as though there were no law against that sort of thing in the world.

"There!" cried the highwayman, as he returned after the last item of his loot had been stowed away in the vehicle. "That'll make an interesting tale for Friday morning's papers. It's the biggest haul I've made in forty-eight years. Good-night, sir. When I am safely out of town I'll telegraph the police to come and rescue you from your present awkward position. And let me tell you, if you give them the slightest hint of my personal appearance, by the hopping Harcourt, I'll come back and kill you. See?"

And with that he made off, closing the door behind him, and a moment later I heard his infernal automobile chugging down the drive at full speed. Twelve hours later, in response to a long-distance telephone message from New York, the police came bounding around to the house, and found me tied up and unconscious. The highwayman had at least been true to his word, and, as he had prophesied, the morning papers on Friday were full of the story of the most daring robbery of the century. Accurate stories in detail under huge scare-type headlines appeared in all the papers, narrating the losses of the Constant-Scrappes, as well as the rape of the jewels and money of Mrs. Van Raffles. The whole country rang with it, and the afternoon train brought not only detectives by the score, but the representative of the Constant-Scrappes and Henriette herself. She was highly hysterical over the loss not only of her own property but that of her landlord as well, but nobody blamed me. The testimony of the police as to my condition when found fully substantiated my story and was accepted as ample evidence that I had no criminal connection with the robbery. This was a great relief to me, but it was greater when Henriette stroked my hand and called me "poor old Bunny," for I must say I was worried as to what she would think of me for having proven so poor a guardian of her property.

Since then months have passed and not a vestige of the stolen property has been recovered. The Constant-Scrappes bore their loss with equanimity, as became them, since no one could have foreseen such a misfortune as overtook them; and as for Mrs. Van Raffles, she never mentioned the matter again to me, save once, and that set me to thinking.

"He was a clever rascal you say, Bunny?" she asked one morning.

"Yes," said I. "One of the best in the business, I fancy."

"A big fellow?" She grinned with a queer smile.

"Oh, about your height," said I.

"Well, by the hopping Harcourt," she retorted, quizzically, "if you give them the slightest hint of *my* personal appearance, I'll come back and kill you. See?"

The man's very words! And then she laughed.

"What?" I cried. "It was—you!"

"Was it?" she returned, airily.

"Why the devil you should go to all that trouble, when you had the stuff right here is what puzzles me," said I.

"Oh, it wasn't any trouble," she replied. "Just sport—you looked so funny sitting up there in your pajamas; and, besides, a material fact such as that hold-up is apt to be more convincing to the police, to say nothing of the Constant-Scrappes, than any mere story we could invent."

"Well, you'd better be careful, Henriette," I said with a shiver. "The detectives are clever—"

"True, Bunny," she answered, gravely. "But you see the highwayman was a man and—well, I'm a woman, dear. I can prove an alibi. By-the-way, you left the cellar-door unlocked that Wednesday. I found it open when I sneaked in to cut off the electric lights. You mustn't be so careless, dear, or we may have to divvy up our spoil with others."

Marvellous woman, that Henriette!

———————————————————————

X
THE ADVENTURE OF MRS. SHADD'S MUSICALE

Henriette was visibly angry the other morning when I took to her the early mail and she discovered that Mrs. Van Varick Shadd had got ahead of her in the matter of Jockobinski, the monkey virtuoso. Society had been very much interested in the reported arrival in America of this wonderfully talented simian who could play the violin as well as Ysaye, and who as a performer on the piano was vastly the superior of Paderewski, because, taken in his infancy and specially trained for the purpose, he could play with his feet and tail as well as with his hands. It had been reported by Tommy Dare, the leading Newport authority on monkeys, that he had heard him play Brahm's "Variations on Paganini" with his paws on a piano, "Hiawatha" on a xylophone with his feet, and "Home, Sweet Home" with his tail on a harp simultaneously, in Paris a year ago, and that alongside of Jockobinski all other musical prodigies of the age became mere strummers.

"He's a whole orchestra in himself," said Tommy enthusiastically, "and is the only living creature that I know of who can tackle a whole symphony without the aid of a hired man."

Of course society was on the *qui vive* for a genius of so riotous an order as this, and all the wealthy families of Newport vied with one another for the privilege of being first to welcome him to our shores, not because he was a freak, mind you, but "for art's sweet sake." Mrs. Gushington-Andrews offered twenty-five hundred dollars for him as a week-end guest, and Mrs. Gaster immediately went her bid a hundred per cent. better. Henriette, in order to outdo every one else, promptly put in a bid of ten thousand dollars for a single evening, and had supposed the bargain closed when along came Mrs. Shadd's cards announcing that she would be pleased to have Mrs. Van Raffles at Onyx House on Friday evening, August 27th, to meet Herr Jockobinski, the eminent virtuoso.

"It's very annoying," said Henriette, as she opened and read the invitation. "I had quite set my heart on having Jockobinski here. Not that I care particularly about the music end of it, but because there is nothing that gives a woman so assured a social position as being the hostess of an animal of his particular kind. You remember, Bunny, how completely Mrs. Shadd wrested the leadership from Mrs. Gaster two seasons ago with her orang outang dinner, don't you?"

I confessed to having read something about such an incident in high society.

"Well," said Henriette, "*this* would have thrown that little episode wholly in the shade. Of course Mrs. Shadd is doing this to retain her grip, but it irritates me more than I can say to have her get it just the same. Heaven knows I was willing to pay for it if I had to abscond with a national bank to get the money."

"It isn't too late, is it?" I queried.

"Not too late?" echoed Henriette. "Not too late with Mrs. Shadd's cards out and the whole thing published in the papers?"

"It's never too late for a woman of your resources to do anything she has a mind to do," said I. "It seems to me that a person who could swipe a Carnegie library the way you did should have little difficulty in lifting a musicale. Of course I don't know how you could do it, but with *your* mind—well, I should be surprised and disappointed if you couldn't devise some plan to accomplish your desires."

Henriette was silent for a moment, and then her face lit up with one of her most charming smiles.

"Bunny, do you know that at times, in spite of your supreme stupidity, you are a source of positive inspiration to me?" she said, looking at me, fondly, I ventured to think.

"I am glad if it is so," said I. "Sometimes, dear Henriette, you will find the most beautiful flowers growing out of the blackest mud. Perhaps hid in the dull residuum of my poor but honest gray matter lies the seed of real genius that will sprout the loveliest blossoms of achievement."

"Well, anyhow, dear, you have started me thinking, and maybe we'll have Jockobinski at Bolivar Lodge yet," she murmured. "I want to have him first, of course, or not at all. To be second in doing a thing of that kind is worse than never doing it at all."

Days went by and not another word was spoken on the subject of Jockobinski and the musicale, and I began to feel that at last Henriette had reached the end of her ingenuity—though for my own part I could not blame her if she failed to find some plausible way out of her disappointment. Wednesday night came, and, consumed by curiosity to learn just how the matter stood, I attempted to sound Henriette on the subject.

"I should like Friday evening off, Mrs. Van Raffles," said I. "If you are going to Mrs. Shadd's musicale you will have no use for me."

"Shut up, Bunny," she returned, abruptly. "I shall need you Friday night more than ever before. Just take this note over to Mrs. Shadd this evening and leave it—mind you, don't wait for an answer but just leave it, that's all."

She arose from the table and handed me a daintily scented missive addressed to Mrs. Shadd, and I faithfully executed her errand. Bunderby, the Shadd's butler, endeavored to persuade me to wait for an answer, but assuring him that I wasn't aware that an answer was expected I returned to Bolivar Lodge. An hour later Bunderby appeared at the back door and handed me a note addressed to my mistress, which I immediately delivered.

"Is Bunderby waiting?" asked Henriette as she read the note.

"Yes," I answered.

"Tell him to hand this to Mrs. Shadd the very first thing upon her return to-morrow evening," she said, hastily scribbling off a note and putting it in an envelope, which by chance she left unsealed, so that on my way back below-stairs I was able to read it. What it said was that she would be only too happy to oblige Mrs. Shadd, and was very sorry indeed to hear that her son had been injured in an automobile accident while running into Boston from Bar Harbor. It closed with the line, "you must know, my dear Pauline, that there isn't anything I wouldn't do for you, come weal or come woe."

This I handed to Bunderby and he made off. On my return Henriette was dressed for travel.

"I must take the first train for New York," she said, excitedly. "You will have the music-room prepared at once, Bunny. Mrs. Shadd's musicale will be given here. I am going myself to make all the necessary arrangements at the New York end. All you have to do is to get things ready and rely on your ignorance for everything else. See?"

I could only reflect that if a successful issue were dependent upon my ignorance I had a plentiful supply of it to fall back on. Henriette made off at once for Providence by motor-car, and got the midnight train out of Boston for the city where, from what I learned afterwards, she must have put in a strenuous day on Thursday. At any rate, a great sensation was sprung on Newport on Friday morning. Every member of the smart set in the ten-o'clock mail received a little engraved card stating that owing to sudden illness in the Shadd family the Shadd musicale for that evening would be held at Bolivar Lodge instead of in the Onyx House ballroom. Friday afternoon Jockobinski's private and particular piano arrived at the Lodge and was set up promptly in the music-room, and later when the caterers arrived with the supper for the four hundred odd guests bidden to the feast all was in readiness for them. Everything was running smoothly, and, although Henriette had not yet arrived, I felt easy and secure of mind until nearing five-thirty o'clock when Mrs. Shadd herself drove up to the front-door. Her color was unusually high, and had she been any but a lady of the *grande monde* I should have said that she was flustered.

She demanded rather than asked to see my mistress, with a hauteur born of the arctic snow.

"Mrs. Van Raffles went to New York Wednesday evening," said I, "and has not yet returned. I am expecting her every minute, madame. She must be here for the musicale. Won't you wait?"

"Indeed I will," said she, abruptly. "The musicale, indeed! Humph!" And she plumped herself down in one of the drawing-room chairs so hard that it was as much as I could do to keep from showing some very unbutlerian concern for the safety of the furniture.

I must say I did not envy Henriette the meeting that was in prospect, for it was quite evident that Mrs. Shadd was mad all through. In spite of my stupidity I rather thought I could divine the cause too. She was not kept long in waiting, for ten minutes later the automobile, with Henriette in it, came thundering up the drive. I tried as I let her in to give her a hint of what awaited her, but Mrs. Shadd forestalled me, only however to be forestalled herself.

"Oh, my dear Pauline!" Henriette cried, as she espied her waiting visitor. "It is *so* good of you to come over. I'm pretty well fagged out with all the arrangements for the night and I *do* hope your son is better."

"My son is not ill, Mrs. Van Raffles," said Mrs. Shadd, coldly. "I have come to ask you what—"

"Not ill?" cried Henriette, interrupting her. "Not ill, Pauline? Why,"— breathlessly—"that's the most extraordinary thing I ever heard of. Why am *I* giving the musicale to-night then, instead of you?"

"That is precisely what I have come to find out," said Mrs. Shadd.

"Why—well, of all queer things," said Henriette, flopping down in a chair. "Surely, you got my note saying that I would let Jockobinski play here to-night instead of—"

"I did receive a very peculiar note from you saying that you would gladly do as I wished," said Mrs. Shadd, beginning herself to look less angry and more puzzled.

"In reply to your note of Wednesday evening," said Henriette. "Certainly you wrote to me Wednesday evening? It was delivered by your own man, Blunderby I think his name is? About half-past seven o'clock it was— Wednesday."

"Yes, Bunderby did carry a note to you from me on Wednesday," said Mrs. Shadd. "But—"

"And in it you said that you were called to Boston by an accident to your son Willie in his automobile: that you might not be able to get back in time for to-night's affair and wouldn't I take it over," protested Mrs. Van Raffles, vehemently.

"I?" said Mrs. Shadd, showing more surprise than was compatible with her high social position.

"And attend to all the details—your very words, my dear Pauline," said Henriette, with an admirably timed break in her voice. "And I did, and *I told you I would.* I immediately put on my travelling gown, motored to Providence, had an all-night ride to New York on a very uncomfortable sleeper, went at once to Herr Jockobinski's agent and arranged the change, notified Sherry to send the supper to my house instead of yours, drove to Tiffany's and had the cards rushed through and mailed to everybody on your list—you know you kindly gave me your list when I first came to Newport—and attended to the whole thing, and now I come back to find it all a—er—a mistake! Why, Pauline, it's positively awful! What *can* we do?"

Henriette was a perfect picture of despair. "I don't suppose we can do anything now," said Mrs. Shadd, ruefully. "It's too late. The cards have gone to everybody. You have all the supper—not a sandwich has come to my house—and I presume all of Mr. Jockobinski's instruments as well have come here."

Henriette turned to me.

"All, madame," said I, briefly.

"Well," said Mrs. Shadd, tapping the floor nervously with her toe. "I don't understand it. *I never* wrote that note."

"Oh, but Mrs. Shadd—I have it here," said Henriette, opening her purse and extracting the paper. "You can read it for yourself. What else could I do after that?"

Innocence on a monument could have appeared no freer of guile than Henriette at that moment. She handed the note to Mrs. Shadd, who perused it with growing amazement.

"Isn't that your handwriting—and your crest and your paper?" asked Henriette, appealingly.

"It certainly looks like it," said Mrs. Shadd. "If I didn't know I *hadn't* written it I would have sworn I had. Where could it have come from?"

"I supposed it came from Onyx House," said Henriette simply, glancing at the envelope.

"Well—it's a very mysterious affair," said Mrs. Shadd, rising, "and I—oh, well, my dear woman, I—I can't blame you—indeed, after all you have done I ought to be—and really am—very much obliged to you. Only—"

"Whom did you have at dinner Wednesday night, dear?" asked Henriette.

"Only the Duke and Duchess of Snarleyow and—mercy! I wonder if he could have done it!"

"Who?" asked Henriette.

"*Tommy Dare!*" ejaculated Mrs. Shadd, her eyes beginning to twinkle. "Do you suppose this is one of Tommy Dare's jokes?"

"H'm!" mused Henriette, and then she laughed. "It wouldn't be unlike him, would it?"

"Not a bit, the naughty boy!" cried Mrs. Shadd. "That's it, Mrs. Van Raffles, as certainly as we stand here. Suppose, just to worry him, we never let on that anything out of the ordinary has happened, eh?"

"Splendid!" said Henriette, with enthusiasm. "Let's act as if all turned out just as we expected, and, best of all, *never even mention it to him, or to Bunderby his confederate, neither of us, eh?*"

"Never!" said Mrs. Shadd, rising and kissing Henriette good-bye. "That's the best way out of it. If we did we'd be the laughing-stock of all Newport. But some day in the distant future Tommy Dare would better look out for Pauline Shadd, Mrs. Van Raffles."

And so it was agreed, and Henriette successfully landed Mrs. Shadd's musicale.

Incidentally, Jockobinski was very affable and the function went off well. Everybody was there and no one would for a moment have thought that there was anything strange in the transfer of the scene from Onyx House to Bolivar Lodge.

"Who wrote that letter, Henriette?" I asked late in the evening when the last guest had gone.

"Who do you suppose, Bunny, my boy?" she asked with a grin. "Bunderby?"

"No," said I.

"You've guessed right," said Henriette.

As a postscript let me say that until he reads this I don't believe Tommy Dare ever guessed what a successful joke he perpetrated upon Mrs. Shadd and the fair Henriette. Even then I doubt if he realizes what a good one it was on—everybody.

XI
THE ADVENTURE OF MRS. INNITT'S COOK

"It is curious, Bunny," said Henriette the other morning after an unusually late breakfast, "to observe by what qualities certain of these Newport families have arrived, as the saying is. The Gasters of course belong at the top by patent right. Having invented American society, or at least the machine that at present controls it, they are entitled to all the royalties it brings in. The Rockerbilts got there all of a sudden by the sheer lavishness of their entertainment and their ability to give bonds to keep it up. The Van Varick Shadds flowed in through their unquestioned affiliation with the ever-popular Delaware Shadds and the Roe-Shadds of the Hudson, two of the oldest and most respected families of the United States, reinforced by the Napoleonic qualities of the present Mrs. Shadd in the doing of unexpected things. The Gullets, thanks to the fact that Mrs. Gullet is the acknowledged mother-in-law of three British dukes, two Italian counts, and a French marquis, are safely anchored in the social haven where they would be, and the rumor that Mrs. Gushington-Andrews has written a book that is a trifle risque fixes her firmly in the social constellation—but the Innitts with only eighty thousand dollars per annum, the Dedbroke-Hickses with nothing a year, the Oliver-Sloshingtons with an income of judgments, the study of their arrival is mighty interesting."

"It doesn't interest me much," quoth I. "Indeed, this American smart set don't appeal to me either for its smartness or its setness."

"Bunny!" cried Henriette, with a silvery ripple of laughter. "Do be careful. An epigram from you? My dear boy, you'll be down with brain-fever if you don't watch out."

"Humph!" said I, with a shrug of my shoulders. "Neither you nor my dear old friend Raffles ever gave me credit for any brains. I have a few, however, which I use when occasion demands," I drawled.

"Well, don't waste them here, Bunny," laughed Henriette. "Save 'em for some place where they'll be appreciated. Maybe in your old age you'll be back in dear old London contributing to *Punch* if you are careful of your wits. But how do you suppose the Oliver-Sloshingtons ever got in here?"

"He holds the divorce record I believe," said I. "He's been married to four social leaders already, hasn't he?"

"Yes—"

"Well, he got into the swim with each marriage—so he's got a four-ply grip," said I.

"And the Dedbroke-Hickses?" asked Henriette. "How do you account for them?"

"Most attractive diners and weekenders," said I. "They got all the laughs at your dinner to the Archbishop of Decanterbury, and their man Smathers tells me they're the swellest things going at week-end parties because of his ingenuity at cotillion leading and her undeniable charms as a flirt. By Jove! she's that easy with men that even I tremble with anxiety whenever she comes into the house."

"But how do they live?—they haven't a cent to their names," said Henriette.

"Simplicity itself," said I. "He is dressed by his tailors and she by her dressmaker; and as for food, they take home a suit-case full of it from every house-party they attend. They're so gracious to the servants that they don't have to think of tips; and as for Smathers, and Mrs. Dedbroke-Hicks's maid, they're paid reporters on the staff of *The Town Tattler* and are willing to serve for nothing for the opportunities for items the connection gives them."

"Well—I don't envy them in the least," said Henriette. "Poor things—to be always taking and never giving must be an awful strain, though to be sure their little trolley party out to Tiverton and back was delightful—"

"Exactly; and with car-fare and sandwiches, and the champagne supplied free by the importers, for the advertisement, it cost them exactly twelve dollars and was set down as the jolliest affair of the season," said I. "I call that genius of a pretty high order. I wouldn't pity them if I were you. They're happy."

"Mrs. Innitt, though—I envy her," said Henriette; "that is, in a way. She has no conversation at all, but her little dinners are the swellest things of the season. Never more than ten people at a time and everything cooked to a turn."

"That's just it," said I. "I hear enough at the club to know just what cinches Mrs. Innitt's position. It's her cook, that's what does it. If she lost her cook she'd be Mrs. Outofit. There never were such pancakes, such purées, such made dishes as that woman gets up. She turns hash into a confection and liver and bacon into a delicacy. Corned-beef in her hands is a discovery and her sauces are such that a bit of roast rhinoceros hide tastes like the tenderest of squab when served by her. No wonder Mrs. Innitt holds her own. A woman with a cook like Norah Sullivan could rule an empire."

A moment later I was sorry I had spoken, for my words electrified her.

"*I must have her!*" cried Henriette.

"What, Mrs. Innitt?" I asked.

"No—her cook," said Henriette.

I stood aghast. Full of sympathy as I had always been with the projects of Mrs. Van Raffles, and never in the least objecting on moral grounds to any of her schemes of acquisition, I could not but think that this time she proposed to go too far. To rob a millionaire of his bonds, a national bank of its surplus, a philanthropist of a library, or a Metropolitan Boxholder of a diamond stomacher, all that seemed reasonable to me and proper according to my way of looking at it, but to rob a neighbor of her cook—if there is any worse social crime than that I don't know what it is.

"You'd better think twice on that proposition, Henriette," I advised with a gloomy shake of the head. "It is not only a mean crime, but a dangerous one to boot. Success would in itself bring ruin. Mrs. Innitt would never forgive you, and society at large—"

"Society at large would dine with me instead of with Mrs. Innitt, that's all," said Henriette. "I mean to have her before the season's over."

"Well, I draw the line at stealing a cook," said I, coldly. "I've robbed churches and I've made way with fresh-air funds, and I've helped you in many another legitimate scheme, but in this, Mrs. Van Raffles, you'll have to go it alone."

"Oh, don't you be afraid, Bunny," she answered. "I'm not going to use your charms as a bait to lure this culinary Phyllis into the Arcadia in which you with your Strephonlike form disport yourself."

"You oughtn't to do it at all," said I, gruffly. "It's worse than murder, for it is prohibited twice in the decalogue, while murder is only mentioned once."

"What!" cried Henrietta "What, pray, does the decalogue say about cooks, I'd like to know?"

"First, thou shalt not steal. You propose to steal this woman. Second, thou shalt not covet thy neighbor's maid-servant. How many times does that make?" I asked.

"Dear me, Bunny," said Henriette, "but you *are* a little tuppenny Puritan, aren't you? Anybody'd know you were the son of a clergyman! Well, let me tell you, I sha'n't steal the woman, and I sha'n't covet her. I'm just going to get her, that's all."

It was two weeks later that Norah Sullivan left the employ of Mrs. Innitt and was installed in our kitchen; and, strange to relate, she came as a matter of charity on Henriette's part—having been discharged by Mrs. Innitt.

The Friday before Norah's arrival Henriette requested me to get her a rusty nail, a piece of gravel from the drive, two hair-pins, and a steel nut from the automobile.

"What on earth—" I began, but she shut me off with an imperious gesture.

"Do as I tell you," she commanded. "You are not in on this venture." And then apparently she relented. "But I'm willing to tell you just one thing, Bunny"—here her eyes began to twinkle joyously—"I'm going to Mrs. Innitt's to dinner to-morrow night—so look out for Norah by Monday."

I turned sulkily away.

"You know how I feel on that subject," said I. "This business of going into another person's house as a guest and inducing their servants to leave is an infraction of the laws of hospitality. How would you like it if Mrs. Gaster stole me away from you?"

Henriette's answer was a puzzling smile. "You are free to better your condition, Bunny," she said. "But I am not going to rob Mrs. Innitt, as I told you once before. She will discharge Norah and I will take her, that's all; so do be a good boy and bring me the nail and gravel and the hair-pins and the automobile nut."

I secured the desired articles for my mistress, and the next evening she went to Mrs. Innitt's little dinner to Miss Gullet and her fiancé, Lord Dullpate, eldest son of the Duke of Lackshingles, who had come over to America to avoid the scrutiny of the Bankruptcy Court, taking the absurd objects with her. Upon her return at 2 A.M. she was radiant and triumphant.

"I won out, Bunny—I won out!" she cried.

"How?" I inquired.

"Mrs. Innitt has discharged Norah, though I begged her not to," she fairly sang.

"On what grounds?"

"Several," said Henriette, unfastening her glove. "To begin with, there was a rusty nail in my clam cocktail, and it nearly choked me to death. I tried hard to keep Mrs. Innitt from seeing what had happened, but she is watchful if not brainy, and all my efforts went for naught. She was much mortified of course and apologized profusely. All went well until the fish, when one of the two hair-pins turned up in the pompano to the supreme disgust of my hostess, who was now beginning to look worried. Hair-pin number two made its début in my timbale. This was too much for the watchful Mrs. Innitt, self-poised though she always is, and despite my remonstrances she excused herself from the table for a moment, and I judge from the flushed appearance of her cheeks when she returned five minutes later that somebody had had the riot act read to her somewhere.

"'I don't understand it at all, Mrs. Van Raffles,' she said with a sheepish smile. 'Cook's perfectly sober. If anything of the kind ever happens again she shall go.'"

"ON HER WAY TO BARLY CHURCH I WAYLAID NORAH"

"Even as Mrs. Innitt spoke I conveyed a luscious morsel of filet mignon with mushrooms to my mouth and nearly broke my tooth on a piece of gravel that went with it, and Norah was doomed, for although we all laughed heartily, the thing had come to be such a joke, it was plain from the expression of Mrs. Innitt's countenance that she was very, very angry.

"'Forgive her this time for my sake, Mrs. Innitt,' I pleaded. 'After all it is the little surprises that give zest to life.'"

"And you didn't have to use the automobile nut?" I asked, deeply impressed with the woman's ingenuity.

"Oh yes," said Henriette. "As dinner progressed I thought it wise to use it to keep Mrs. Innitt from weakening; so when the salad was passed I managed, without anybody's observing it, to drop the automobile nut into the bowl. The Duke of Snarleyow got it and the climax was capped. Mrs. Innitt burst into a flood of tears and—well, to-morrow, Bunny, Norah leaves. You will take her this ten-dollar bill from me, and tell her that I am sorry she got into so much trouble on my account. Say that if I can be of any assistance to her all she has to do is to call here and I will do what I can to get her another place."

With this Henriette retired and the next morning on her way to early church I waylaid Norah. Her eyes were red with weeping, but a more indignant woman never lived. Her discharge was unrighteous; Mrs. Innitt was no lady; the butler was in a conspiracy to ruin her—and all that; indeed, her mood was most receptive to the furtherance of Henriette's plans. The ten-dollar bill was soothing, and indicated that my mistress was a "foine woman" and "surely Norah would come 'round in the evening to ask her aid."

"It's ruined I am unless somebody'll be good to me and give me a riference, which Mrs. Innitt, bad cess to her, won't do, at all, at all," she wailed, and then I left her.

She called that night, and two days later was installed in the Van Raffles's kitchen.

A new treasure was added to the stores of our loot, but somehow or other I have never been happy over the successful issue of the enterprise. I can't quite make up my mind that it was a lady-like thing for Henriette to do even in Newport.

XII
THE LAST ADVENTURE

I am bathed in tears. I have tried to write of my sensations, to tell the story of the Last Adventure of Mrs. Van Raffles, in lucid terms, but though my pen runs fast over the paper the ink makes no record of the facts. My woe is so great and so deep that my tears, falling into the ink-pot, turn it into a fluid so thin it will not mark the paper, and when I try the pencil the words are scarce put down before they're blotted out. And yet with all this woe I find myself a multi-millionaire—possessed of sums so far beyond my wildest dreams of fortune that my eye can scarce take in the breadth of all the figures. My dollars coined into silver, placed on top of one another, would form a bullion tower that would reach higher into the air than fifteen superimposed domes of St. Peter's placed on top of seventeen spires of Trinity on the summit of Mont Blanc. In five-pound notes laid side by side they'd suffice to paper every scrap of bedroom wall in all the Astor houses in the world, and invested in Amalgamated Copper they would turn the system green with envy—and yet I am not happy. My well-beloved Henriette's last adventure has turned my fortune into bitterest gall, and plain unvarnished wormwood forms the finish of my interior, for she is gone! I, amid the splendor of my new-found possessions, able to keep not one but a hundred motor-cars, and to pay the chauffeur's fines, to endow chairs in universities, to build libraries in every hamlet in the land from Podunk to Richard Mansfield, to eat three meals a day and lodge at the St. Regicide, and to evade my taxes without exciting suspicion, am desolate and forlorn, for, I repeat, Henriette has gone! The very nature of her last adventure by a successful issue has blown out the light of my life.

She has stolen Constant-Scrappe!

If I could be light of heart in this tragic hour I would call this story the Adventure of the Lifted Fiancé, but that would be so out of key with my emotions that I cannot bring myself to do it. I must content myself with a narration of the simple facts of the lengths to which my beloved's ambition led her, without frivolity and with a heavy heart.

Of course you know what all Newport has known for months, that the Constant-Scrappes were seeking divorce, not that they loved one another less, but that both parties to the South Dakota suit loved some one else more. Colonel Scrappe had long been the most ardent admirer of Mrs. Gushington-Andrews, and Mrs. Constant-Scrappe's devotion to young Harry de Lakwitz had been at least for two seasons evident to any observer with half an eye. Gushington-Andrews had considerately taken himself out of the way by eloping to South Africa with Tottie Dimpleton of the Frivolity Burlesquers, and Harry de Lakwitz's only recorded marriage had been annulled by the courts because at the time of his wedding to the forty-year-old housemaid of the Belleville Boarding-School for Boys at Skidgeway, Rhode Island, he was only fifteen years of age. Consequently, they both were eligible, and provided the Constant-Scrappes could be so operated on by the laws of South Dakota as to free them from one another, there were no valid reasons why the yearnings of these ardent souls should not all be gratified. Indeed, both engagements had been announced tentatively, and only the signing of the decree releasing the Constant-Scrappes from their obligations to one another now stood in the way of two nuptial ceremonies which would make four hearts beat as one. Mrs. Gushington-Andrews's trousseau was ready, and that of the future Mrs. de Lakwitz had been ordered; both ladies had received their engagement rings when that inscrutable Henriette marked Constant-Scrappe for her own. Colonel Scrappe had returned from Monte Carlo, having broken the bank twice, and Henriette had met him at a little dinner given in his honor by Mrs. Gushington-Andrews. He turned out to be a most charming man, and it didn't require a much more keen perception than my own to take in the fact that he had made a great impression upon Henriette, though she never mentioned it to me until the final blow came. I merely noticed a growing preoccupation in her manner and in her attitude towards me, which changed perceptibly.

"I think, Bunny," she said to me one morning as I brought her marmalade and toast, "that considering our relations to each other you should not call me Henrietta. After all, you know, you are here primarily as my butler, and there are some proprieties that should be observed even in this Newport atmosphere."

"But," I protested, "am I no more than that? I am your partner, am I not?"

"You are my business partner—not my social, Bunny," she said. "We must not mix society and business. In this house I am mistress of the situation; you are the butler—that is the precise condition, and I think it well that hereafter you should recognize the real truth and avoid over-familiarity by addressing me as Mrs. Van Raffles. If we should ever open an office for our Burglary Company in New York or elsewhere you may call me anything you please there. Here, however, you must be governed by the etiquette of your environment. Let it be *Mrs.* Van Raffles hereafter."

"And is it to be Mr. Bunny?" I inquired, sarcastically.

Her response was a cold glance of the eye and a majestic sweep from the room.

"HENRIETTE WAS TESTING THE FIFTY-THOUSAND-
DOLLAR PIANO"

That evening Colonel Scrappe called, ostensibly to look over the house and as landlord to see if there was anything he could do to make it more comfortable, and I, blind fool that I was for the moment, believed that that was his real errand, and ventured to remind Henriette of the leak in the roof, at which they both, I thought, exchanged amused glances, and *he* gravely mounted the stairs to the top of the house to look at it. On our return, Henriette dismissed me and told me that she would not require my services again during the evening. Even then my suspicions were not aroused, although there was a dull, disturbed feeling about my heart whose precise causes I could not define. I went to the club and put in a miserable evening, returning home about midnight to discover that Colonel Scrappe was still there. He was apparently giving the house and its contents a thorough inspection, for when I arrived, Henriette was testing the fifty-thousand-dollar piano in the drawing-room for him with a brilliant rendering of "O Promise Me." What decision they reached as to its tone and quality I never knew, for in spite of my hints on the subject, Henriette never spoke of the matter to me. I suppose I should have begun to guess what was happening under my very nose then, but thank Heaven I am not of a suspicious nature, and although I didn't like the looks of things, the inevitable meaning of their strange behavior never even dawned upon my mind. Even when two nights later Colonel Scrappe escorted Henriette home at midnight from a lecture on the Inscrutability of Sartor Resartus at Mrs. Gushington-Andrews's it did not strike me as unusual, although, instead of going home immediately, as most escorts do under the circumstances, he remained about two hours testing that infernal piano again, and with the same old tune.

Then the automobile rides began, and pretty nearly every morning, long before polite society was awake, Colonel Scrappe and Henriette took long runs together through the country in her Mercedes machine, for what purpose I snever knew, for whatever interest the colonel might have had in our welfare as a landlord I could not for the life of me guess how it could be extended to our automobiles. One thing I did notice, however, was a growing coldness between Henriette and Mrs. Gushington-Andrews. The latter came to a card-party at Bolivar Lodge one afternoon about two weeks after Colonel Scrappe's return, and her greeting to her hostess instead of having the old-time effusiveness was frigid to a degree. In fact, when they clasped hands I doubt if more than the tips of their fingers touched. Moreover, Mrs. Gushington-Andrews, hitherto considered one of the best fists at bridge or hearts in the 400, actually won the booby prize, which I saw her throw into the street when she departed. It was evident something had happened to disturb her equanimity.

My eyes were finally opened by a remark made at the club by Digby, Reggie de Pelt's valet, who asked me how I liked my new boss, and whose explanation of the question led to a complete revelation of the true facts in the case. Everybody knew, he said, that from the moment she had met him Mrs. Van Raffles had set her cap for Colonel Scrappe, and that meeting her for the first time he had fallen head over heels in love with her even in the presence of his fiancée. Of course I hotly denied Digby's insinuations, and we got so warm over the discussion that when I returned home that night I had two badly discolored eyes, and Digby—well, Digby didn't go home at all. Both of us were suspended from the Gentleman's Gentleman's Club for four weeks for ungentleman's ungentlemanly behavior in consequence. Black as my eyes were, however, I was on hand at the breakfast-table the following morning, and of course Henriette observed my injuries.

"Why, Bunny!" she cried. "What is the meaning of this? Have you been fighting?"

"Oh no, Mrs. Van Raffles," I returned, sarcastically, "I've just strained my eyes reading the divorce news from South Dakota."

She gave a sudden start.

"What do you mean?" she demanded, her face flushing hotly.

"You know well enough what I mean," I retorted, angrily. "Your goings on with Colonel Scrappe are the talk of the town, and I got these eyes in a little discussion of your matrimonial intentions. That's all."

"Leave the room instantly!" she cried, rising and haughtily pointing to the door. "You are insufferable."

But the color in her cheeks showed that I had hit home far harder than she was willing to admit. There was nothing for me to do but to obey meekly, but my blood was up, and instead of moping in my room I started out to see if I could find Constant-Scrappe. My love for Henriette was too deep to permit of my sitting quietly by and seeing another walk away with the one truly coveted prize of my life, and I was ready on sight to take the colonel by the collar—he was only a governor's-staff colonel anyhow, and, consequently no great shakes as a fighter—and throw him into the harbor, but my quest was a vain one. He was to be found in none of his familiar haunts, and I returned to Bolivar Lodge. And then came the shock. As I approached the house I saw the colonel assisting Henriette into the motor-car, and in response to the chauffeur's "Where to, sir," I heard Scrappe reply in an excited undertone:

"To New York—and damn the speed laws."

In a moment they had rushed by me like the flash of a lightning express, and Henriette was gone!

You must know the rest. The papers the next day were full of the elopement in high life. They told how the Scrappe divorce had been granted at five o'clock in the afternoon the day before, how Colonel Scrappe and Mrs. Van Raffles had sped to New York in the automobile and been quietly married at the Little Church Around the Corner, and were now sailing down the bay on the *Hydrostatic*, bound for foreign climes. They likewise intimated that a very attractive lady of more than usual effusiveness of manner, whose nuptials were expected soon to be published for the second time, had gone to a sanitarium in Philadelphia to be treated for a sudden and overwhelming attack of nervous hysteria.

It was all too true, that tale. Henriette's final coup had been successful, and she had at one stroke stolen her landlord, her landlady's husband, and her neighbor's fiancé. To console me she left this note, written on board of the steamer and mailed by the pilot.

ON BOARD THE HYDROSTATIC.
OFF SANDY HOOK, *September 10, 1904.*

DEAR BUNNY,—I couldn't help it. The minute I saw him I felt that I must have him. It's the most successful haul yet and is the last adventure I shall ever have. He's worth forty million dollars. I'm sorry for you, dear, but it's all in the line of business. To console you I have left in your name all that we have won together in our partnership at Newport—fourteen millions five hundred and sixty-three thousand nine hundred and seventy-seven dollars in cash, and about three million dollars in jewels, which you must negotiate carefully. Good-bye, dear Bunny, I shall never forget you, and I wish you all the happiness in the world. With the funds now in your possession why not retire—go home to England and renew your studies for the ministry? The Church is a noble profession.

Sincerely yours,
HENRIETTE VAN RAFFLES-SCRAPPE.

I have gathered together these meagre possessions—rich in bullion value, but meagre in happiness, considering all that might have been, and to-morrow I sail for London. There, following Henriette's advice, I shall enter the study of the ministry, and when I am ordained shall buy a living somewhere and settle down to the serene existence of the preacher, the pastor of a flock of human sheep.

"MY MISERY IS DEEP BUT I AM BUOYED UP BY ONE GREAT HOPE"

My misery is deep but I am buoyed up by one great hope in every thought.

These Newport marriages are so seldom for life that I yet have hope that some day Henriette will be restored to me without its necessarily involving any serious accident to her husband the colonel.

Milton Keynes UK
Ingram Content Group UK Ltd.
UKHW010706240424
441619UK00004B/310